My Illegitimate Son

My
Illegitimate
Son

A True Story

SANJAY JHA

Illustrations by Bhavya

RUPA

Published by
Rupa Publications India Pvt. Ltd 2023
7/16, Ansari Road, Daryaganj
New Delhi 110002

Sales centres:
Prayagraj Bengaluru Chennai
Hyderabad Jaipur Kathmandu
Kolkata Mumbai

Copyright © Sanjay Jha 2023

The views and opinions expressed in this book are the author's own and the facts are as reported by him which have been verified to the extent possible, and the publishers are not in any way liable for the same.

All rights reserved.
No part of this publication may be reproduced, transmitted, or stored in a retrieval system, in any form or by any means, electronic, mechanical, photocopying, recording or otherwise, without the prior permission of the publisher.

P-ISBN: 978-93-5702-094-7
E-ISBN: 978-93-5702-109-8

First impression 2023

10 9 8 7 6 5 4 3 2 1

The moral right of the author has been asserted.

Printed in India

This book is sold subject to the condition that it shall not, by way of trade or otherwise, be lent, resold, hired out, or otherwise circulated, without the publisher's prior consent, in any form of binding or cover other than that in which it is published.

This book is dedicated to all those who have experienced the pain of loss because they are the fortunate ones who have understood what love is.

CONTENTS

Prologue ix

0 Chapter Zero 1
1 Here I Come 7
2 We Have Visitors 15
3 Mama Mia! 23
4 Home With Weirdos 31
5 Hi Olly 39
6 Those Heady Early Days 48
7 The Madness Continues 57
8 The Studs Rule The World 73
9 Middle-Aged And All 83
10 The Visitor 93
11 The Goodbyes Begin 99
12 Soulmates...Forever 107
13 WTH Is WFH 121
14 Pure Magic And Then... 136
15 Home, At Last 145
16 A Letter For My Family 154

Epilogue: One Month Later 178
Acknowledgements 183

PROLOGUE

*'When a man's best friend is his dog,
that dog has a problem.'*
—Edward Abbey

I grew up in a crowded home with three cantankerous siblings born for a bullring, a tempestuous mother who would have made Mount Vesuvius tremble, a father who seemed to be the reincarnation of a spiritual guru in permanent meditation, and several unpredictable dogs with differing poop times. The fact that I somehow miraculously retained my sanity intrigues me to this day. But I have survived to tell this tale.

I am not surprised at chronic cribbers, who call their frequent doomsday sentiment with dismissive disdain as 'a dog's life'. But it is not necessarily accurate. Many of the canine fraternity will remonstrate at that condescending summarization. Some will even react with an indignant facial expression that exposes bright white teeth, albeit in a jovial vein. Certainly, Amadeus would have, I think.

He came home for the first time in the small dashboard in front of the rider's seat in a Bajaj scooter usually reserved for licence papers and a lunch packet. He was so small. He was delivered to us by a garrulous and cunning dog merchandiser who was brokering a sale deal for a pedigree German Shepherd pup to obviously moonstruck customers. Around the same time, we saw the Hollywood classic *Amadeus*, the movie that won nine Oscar Awards, based on the tumultuous life of a musical genius, Wolfgang Amadeus Mozart. It was a compelling watch. My wife and I looked at the small, soft, inscrutable black-haired frisky thing in our hands and thought he possessed all the grandeur of the music icon. He had a mind of his own and made arresting sounds, not necessarily melodious but impactful nevertheless. That's how the name Amadeus came to be.

Amadeus had the luxurious suggestion of the imperial lion king in his mane; a handsome frame, commanding a glistening hirsute hue of golden brown and dark black. The ears stood in perpetual attention, like a German achtung. The side of his finely crafted jaw had a conspicuous dark spot, signifying the distinctive mark of a blue blood. The tail swaggered in rhythmic harmony whenever he smelt cottage cheese, and since non-vegetarian meal was strictly prohibited at home, Amadeus was essentially a reluctant vegetarian who could have done with some red meat. He, of course, gorged on the juicy bones and those assortments of meat-flavoured goodies we bought for him from the friendly neighbourhood store. If he received an occasional hollering for ingeniously transporting some bony remains from the street side, he offered a convincing expression; 'Me Dog, Love bone. Why you guys getting so uptight? Anyway, I forgive you.' For him, that explained the Society for Prevention of Cruelty to Animals. Amadeus could never perhaps fathom why human beings, so intent on self-destruction and mutual antipathy on a regular basis, often diverted their foul intentions on the most benign four-legged creature. To top it all, this gluttonous variety even had the audacity to eat a thing called a hotdog.

Amadeus was essentially in the non-violent pacifist mould, and remarkably serene given his natural inherited Gestapo inclinations when it came to the human race. But when he spotted another competitive tail running around in his territory, he assumed wolfish proportions. He came into an aggressive avatar. It was his own sacrosanct domain and neighbouring dogs were forewarned to stay clear; that was his non-negotiable diktat. In that sense, he was schizophrenic; a Dr Jekyll and Mr Hyde. Once he sniffed up without any pervert intentions the dropping trousers of an unsuspecting visitor, till that poor fellow almost literally hit the ceiling. For all the barbaric, heartless attack that dogs receive at the hands of cruel sadistic humans, this was according to Amadeus, comeuppance, although it was only an innocuous tease. The truth is that if you have a dog who licks your face, you will never need to see a shrink, was what Amadeus wanted to say. But very few of us know this secret unless you are a dog-whisperer perhaps.

He loved car rides so much, I believe he would have loved to be in the driver's seat, with an authorised licence from the RTO (Regional Transport Office) to boot. Going back and forth to Pune, he would stand upright even as the car bumped along the expansive highways, his heavy breathing resonating in the car. For him, this was the open space that a journey provided, away from the unbearable excesses of the metropolitan madness that was his life in Mumbai. Occasionally, I would watch him look at the traffic snarls from our second-floor residence, as if he wondered why the teeming nitwits were so clueless about work-life balance. Why this utter chaos, the incessant honking, the frenetic pace? I think he almost shook his head in acute disbelief and profuse sympathy for us: 'These guys suffer from road rage, and they call mine with choleric contempt as a dog's life? Really?' He was so right.

He walked with imposing strides, loved the early morning stretch, and did complex poses, head lowered, front legs bent at 45 degrees and back legs straightened without a muscle twitch. I am sure he wondered why we made such a big deal about emerging from a similar routine with a triumphant expression as if we had climbed Mount Everest. Unmindful of the Sensex volatility, slumping economy, communal tensions, cacophonic TV debates, and celebrity gossip in Page 3 columns, he snoozed and slept his way through his daily travails. He needed no stress-busters, but that irritating sneaky Beagle did occasionally get under his skin. Amadeus did not need to read *How to Stop Worrying and Start Living*. Or listen to an Anthony Robbins podcast. Or sing paeans of Oprah Winfrey. Not Amadeus. You take your warm baths and get the fragrance right to keep the insomnia out, folks, I sleep just fine is what he said. Then he snored.

Amadeus adored my two girls, allowing them to indulgently create havoc with him, make a mess of his afternoon nap sessions, put him through some fashion experiments, and even have him wear branded apparel in winter. But he never ever complained. They adored him.

It was a pulp non-fiction of foamy mush and bonding of the souls between them.

One regular day at exactly 11.07 a.m., he passed away. Almost as quietly as he had arrived in the palm of a hand twelve and a half years ago. He had been battling an internal condition for over two weeks that had suddenly consumed his already depleted energy and strong reserves. Over the preceding few months, the big jump at the door had transformed to a slower wag and a half-hearted lurch. Now he preferred to be smothered; his tiring legs prevented him from even making his customary call at the door. The big wide smile was still there as was the unbridled happiness of seeing us all home. But a spate of illnesses had become regular. The decline was perceptible. He watched you come in from a distance, his own legs were far too enervated now to traverse the distance with his customary swagger. It was time to do a Google search on average life expectancy of a German Shepherd. It said 12-13 years.

I remember taking a walk down the back-lane the day after he said adieu, where we hung out together. His favourite locations, his penchant for following a process for his dump. A sniff. A circle. A sniff. Two circles. And then indecision. I remembered it all. I looked around at all the places at home where he ensconced himself in his magnificent pose, guarding the entire household with his alert eyes. At meal times, his favourite vessel was empty. That comforting smell of boiled basmati rice from his body was not in the air. His walking leash lay on the shelf untouched because it had nowhere to go. When one heard a distant bark, I almost thought he was around.

Or perhaps never gone. And I looked for those large brown eyes somewhere, speaking a million nuances, with just a longer lingering stare. Or the unrestrained gleam of joy. Of love, that was not measured, and did not fear your absence of reciprocity. Of that acceptance of loneliness when we would leave him alone during our summer holidays. Or the pain of an end that he knew was inevitable.

Our home looked sparkless, the overcaffeinated energy was gone overnight, and a dreary silence pervaded. Death is brutal. Even when you know it is as certain as the GST, when it hits you, it is like a big bus crushing you under its mammoth weight. The morning after is the worst, I think, because you wake up to a world without the one you lost. It feels weird, leaving you numb, clueless about what to do, and severely broken as if someone has cut a part of your limb. And yet life must go on. We must eat, drink, sleep, work, and watch a TV serial, and before we realize it, start laughing again. I also ran.

It was a Mumbai winter evening; the skies were greyish with a mix of carbon dioxide and an unusually dense fog. Running is therapeutic, and while your mind can still clobber you with garbage, it mostly succeeds in keeping you on track. At the Race Course, one of the few open public spaces in the city where you could breathe, I normally rediscovered myself, free of the monkeys chattering away on my shoulders. I had just turned the bend at my fastest pace, behind which was a towering skyscraper, when I momentarily froze, before I stopped altogether. Now what the hell was that? Was it a giant lizard or a bloated slug? Was it an Animal Planet freak show or just an optical illusion?

To answer these questions, it took a while. Frankly, nearly thirteen years. That miniature contraption on a leash would inspire an upending of our lives, turning it upside down, quintessentially topsy-turvy. As you will soon find out, we had a Yoda of sorts on our hand. And a storyteller.

0

CHAPTER ZERO

> 'My fashion philosophy is,
> if you are not covered in dog hair, your life is empty.'
> —Elayne Boosler

I have never understood the human fascination for a dog's anal passage. Honestly, we may walk around in the buff, but these guys are serious perverts. And they pontificate on the right to privacy! Huh! Why do I start by sounding so pissed? Well, there's a reason. I just woke up, blurry-eyed, my heart palpitating wildly, feeling unusually breathless and with a particularly searing pain in my stomach. I have never felt so disoriented, so discombobulated in my whole twelve and a half years of existence despite surviving these neurotic types on two legs. Never. Despite my own family, honestly; they sure are a weird bunch. Even from a distance measured between my two ears they speak so loudly you would think that the unpredictable maverick from North Korea had just launched a nuclear missile to wrap up his birthday celebrations. I have highly sensitive ears (which is why I avoid prime-time cable TV), and their cacophonous conversations are a reminder of those deadly nights when they burst crackers and dance to some awful music while wearing gaudy clothes and gorging saturated fats aplenty. Religious celebrations give them a free license, clearly. Like several historical monuments in the second most populous country in the world that I live in, I too am a clearly disputed structure. You see, everything eventually gets hotly political. They quibble all the time over who loves me more, who volunteers to take me out for my daily constitutional and patiently waits outside the clinic when some patsy fellow wearing a mask to conceal his bad breath keeps poking my tummy, et cetera, et cetera. So far so good, and I enjoy the social tensions that my presence invariably causes. But strangely, no one has ever bothered to ask me that question: 'Do I have a first among equals? Or am I a true-blue liberal, which cannot be said of many in that hilarious ecosystem comprising so many crackpots.' Anyway, as usual, I am digressing. 'Right now, what I cannot fathom is what am I doing in this wretched place with the smell of an ominous, suffocating disinfectant?' I need answers. I need them now. And I am clueless. 'Not good, this. Not good at all.'

My temper now rose from the depths of a V-curve. 'Where the hell is my dearest mama?' This was not the time for answering emails, for god's sake, or doing a conference call with funny faces trapped forever in a dog cage. Zoom, my left paw! And that exasperating father of mine who thinks I can be fooled by his syrupy sing-song hymn 'Lou-cha-pa', which I believe is an awful wordplay at giving my aristocratic French name Louis a peculiar Chinese twist. Stupid, because he was among the notorious first who had the damn Covid-19 when the world was still figuring out whether to call it a flu that could be cured by injecting a detergent as suggested by a powerful fellow with messy orange hair, or a Wuhan BatManchu or some other alphanumeric riddle. 'And where are my sweetest two sisters when I need them so frantically?' Well, they must be busy on that slim black instrument that makes their fingers dance while they sport an inscrutable smile on their pretty faces while texting. The younger one usually sweet-talks me every day before shoving an unpalatable sickening syrup down my throat. I know her tricks, although she thinks I am brainless enough to fall for her artifice all the time just because I demonstrate gentlemanly compliance. Huh! I am a master at playing dumb. The elder one talks to me on a mobile phone video every week while wearing a furry cap with vanilla ice cream raining behind her. 'Why would you go to Alaska, dear? Or some frozen dessert called Toronto? Wouldn't being in front of me be a lot easier? Seriously, where was this lunatic bunch?' Instead of waltzing to my wish list, they had abandoned me and allowed this creepy fellow in blue overalls to look at me as if I was a cat; that hurts our aristocratic fraternity. That is intolerably disrespectful. And worse, he carried a thermometer that I knew would soon be in my bum. A sick man, this weirdo, taking full advantage of the fact that my family was in a deep sleep somewhere else. In normal circumstances, I would have probably bitten off one-fourth of his balls if he came even two feet close to me (I will not reveal my actual size to you yet). But as I looked around me quickly, letting my eyes dart across the stannic cage, I knew something was not all right. The rancid smell of chemical acids and a fellow bro in the adjoining chamber whining in acute pain convinced me that me being alone in this abject place, alone, was not an ordinary happenstance. I knew deep in my heart that the lunatics loved me like I love fried eggs with a gooey yolk, with or without cheese. They would not leave me alone. Ever. Or would they?

I was in a hospital. We all hated this ominous sanitized chamber of horrors. That was not good news as I found doctors crocodilian, far from reassuring based on my past experiences. 'Hmmm... My parents know I hate this horrendous place enormously, so why have they suddenly punished me?' It made no sense whatsoever. I was in a bad headspace, as you can make out. I am repeating myself. I am talking to myself. And no one is talking back to me. Worry, bro!

There was a deathly stillness around and the mercury lights emanating from across the passageway felt unusually dark to me. It did not help that the painkillers were like psychedelic drugs, playing truant with my over-imaginative mind. I watched the creep with frizzy hair, thin-rimmed spectacles and an assumed air of self-importance come close to me and shift my position wherein my arse faced him. It hurt. The lazy moron could have easily moved himself behind me instead. But as they say every dog has his day. I would wait my turn. I felt a pointed six-inch glass capsule enter my bum. Thankfully, the creep had at least been gentle in exercising his pathological fetish. Then as all these doctors do, he began examining my shit which had accompanied the thermometer on its way out. Trust me, it is so incomprehensible to me as to how my poo means so much to these quacks. But as he looked at the thermometer more closely, I could see his eyes squint and a deep frown envelop his cherubic face. He looked worried. Since my face was totally immobilized, I strained my eyes to see if I could catch a glimpse of what he had observed. About a fourth of the thermometer was red in colour. I was bleeding. I was in trouble. Heck, it was time to get real, I was in a serious funk. The damn hospital was a doghouse. I had to get out of here fast. But how?

I have no idea how I got here in the first place, and that is saying a lot because I have a phenomenal memory (I hide my bones and can retrieve them weeks later even if I have a stuffed nose). Because all I remembered was that earlier that morning the whole house was abuzz with excitement because we were travelling together in a few hours. And I was thrilled too. There is nothing more exhilarating than letting the breeze hit my face as the car gathers speed on an expressway without those nasty bumps and the intermittent red lights that obstruct my reverie. I feel one with the universe at that time. Life is beautiful. My worries blow away with the wind. So you can imagine my excitement at the journey. I was as thrilled as a dog can be with two tails. I ran out to join the action, unsure about which of the two cars I would be in. I am big so I secretly hoped that I would be in the sleek blue sedan. I went sniffing around and gave the car's tyres my traditional pee shower. That is a ritual that ensures an auspicious start. I turned to see whether mom had packed my tennis balls in, after all I was no less than that

Novak or Roger or Rafa types. It was then that I suddenly heard an angry menacing sound. I had barely registered the source of the fury, when... This is where I blank out, as if in a delirious daze. I have no idea what happened, and what brought me here. Nothing. Nothing at all. It is a blur, like a foggy windscreen on a winter morning drive. And I do not like second-guessing. I am hopelessly incapable of recollecting anything else. Nothing. But when I do wake up, I will tell you for sure. It is a promise. Because otherwise this narrative about someone whom they affectionately called a smoked sausage will never end. It is the missing card of the jigsaw puzzle. I hope you are not panicking while reading this, because what you must not forget is that while everything has an end, only a sausage has two. This story has just begun. So just sit back and join me in a roller-coaster ride.

My eyes are now hard to open as I am clearly given the same white wine that makes mama dance wild, laugh uncontrollably in a hysterical frenzy and then puke the whole night afterwards on New Year's day. Now I know what catatonic means. As my eyes close involuntarily, however, I suddenly begin to remember how it all began. My journey, my entering a madhouse that would become my beloved home. How a toothy bespectacled girl with a squeaky voice saw my tangled tail and pointing at me gave a shriek of joy. We made eye contact and I, the humongous alpha male among several of my tiny siblings, approved of her decision. It is the beginning of my story. My adventures. My romantic odyssey. My life. The year was 2009, one year after an African-American from Hawaii became the most powerful man on earth.

1

HERE I COME

'A baby is nothing more than a loud noise at one end and no sense of responsibility on the other.'
—Ronald Knox

I have a vague memory of my mother. I knew that she was madly in love with this shiny black-haired punk who regretfully looked like me. He had an attitude, as if he was the only one of his kind, the only miniature Dachshund the world had seen, strutting around with his tail parallel to the ground, a sign of both confidence and chutzpah. Some conceit that, though I must concede that I may have inherited some of his immodesty. But surprisingly, it was this cool dude's hubris on his otherwise poker face that seemingly captivated my mother. She fell in love with him hook, line and sinker, floored by his mysterious charms. Quite literally, to be honest. Like adopting a crazy yoga pose on the floor resting on her back, looking moony-eyed at him, while giving him the slightest wag of the tail which continued incessantly for long intervals. She was seducing him for sure but she was in no hurry either. Contradictory? Not really. She was playing hard to get; I guess both humans and dogs read the same romantic 'How To' manuals for dummies. Or a 'How To Hook Up' on a dating app.

It is not the wagging of the tail alone that is a manifestation of our emotional catharsis; it is also its speed of movement from left to right and the frequency of intervals. It is a complex algorithm, frankly. Most humans don't get it. Even Meta won't. Or that maverick Musk.

In our crazy brotherhood, the sex ratio is unfavourably skewed against the she-dog (some of these depraved humans call us 'bitch'). The gender diversity problem is created by, you guessed it right, the human species. Because you find keeping she-dogs a bloody mess, even while you have multiple multinational sanitary brand choices for your monthly mood swings. Truly it is an unfair world. My mother, named Lucy (I assume named after a television celebrity star from yesteryears) by her cranky but doting adopter, clearly knew her prepossessing statistics. She knew there were many suitors, and among them were those named Tom, Dick and Harry too, trust me. I am not trying to be funny.

I have still not understood why many name us dogs as Tigers! Try calling the Lion King 'Tommy' and see what he does to you. Lucy's fan club was a Who's Who. She could have sued every one of them with a hashtag of her own creation, as practically all had wooed her with differing intensity, and some had got carried away with their amorous propensities. One fellow called Dabang stood out because of his straight face and absence of melodramatic histrionics. But he had those sturdy biceps and thick calf muscles that did make my mom drool. He was also a hot-headed rapscallion, it was rumoured, so Lucy eschewed her infatuation. But deep in her heart she was actually smitten by Charlie, who lived on the sixth floor of the sea-facing skyscraper and hung around his balcony to give her sly looks of appreciation, which is a euphemism for insatiable lust. Neither Charlie nor Lucy had a fellow dog companion, as probably humans find managing us little things a gargantuan challenge. Small is beautiful, I guess. At least it is much easier to manage. Anyway, mom would be patient but would let Charlie know that she was interested too. But he had to get rid of his habit of giving those cool dude vibes, as if he was like a trophy acquisition. Alas, Charlie was obdurate and remained b l i t h e l y nonchalant. And arrogant. Because he knew that there was 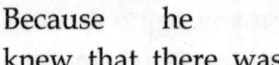 no way a mini-Dachshund could ever mate with anyone else but a mini-Dachshund. You see, at our prime we are about 6 inches tall and weigh 6 kilos, so if we develop amorous inclinations towards a Labrador (or a Beagle too), it would be a bit awkward; like a Chinese bhel. It would be like a bear mating with a butterfly. Dabang for all his masculine oomph and Lucy's crush was a non-starter because while a one-night stand (literally) was a satisfying prospect for Lucy, risking bone-crushing trauma was not on the table. In a way, we mini-Ds are clannish on account of our exceptional lineage. And body metabolism. We don't need no Tinder. We are class conscious in an Oxbridge sort of way.

After rubbing noses, giving each other sidelong glances of our licentious intentions and generally frolicking around, Charlie and my mother eventually fell in love. It helped that Charlie got off his high pedestal after he saw mom being chaperoned by the sturdier folks living in the neck of the woods. Jealousy always works. When Charlie gave Lucy his share of his meaty bone, she knew he was getting serious. Unlike the two-legged species, we are terribly expressive. Moreover, we do not believe in the monotonous instalments of a stolen kiss, hand-holding, some cuddling and petting, before finally revealing our pent-up carnal intentions leading to the final consummation of love. That lengthy masquerade is so unnecessary in our universe.

Charlie licked my mother's face as if she was gooey minced chicken marinated in lamb broth. Mom reciprocated the gesture with fiery gusto. They were now more than just friends. At last. They partied hard, breaking into Charlie's master's cookie jar, which tripped and fell, but since it was made of plastic, there was little damage. Or noise. The solid chunks of chocolate embedded like diamond rings into that circular shaped biscuit was divine, even if they are seemingly taboo for us four-legged wonders for health reasons. What neither Charlie nor Lucy could ever fathom was why these guys ate a jar of such irresistible biscuits in one's and two's. But Charlie was perceptive: 'They become fat. Because all they do is sit and sit and work and work on that silly computer on their laps.' And with a wink he added: 'We run. So let's eat this whole damn thing. Since we will be punished anyway, why not do justice to our efforts?' But Lucy had other ideas: 'Let's not just run. But let's run away for a bit to that quiet neighbourhood behind the bushes of Mr Percy Mistry's home. I want to be with you alone for some time, Charlie.' So after smothering their burps, avoiding water so as to let the taste of cocoa linger,

Charlie and Lucy surreptitiously sneaked into the largely unused compound of Mr Mistry. They could hear Percy barking at his house help for adding too little cheese to his double-fried omelette. They could see the silhouette of his sharp crooked nose and skullcap in the shadows as he paced agitatedly in the large veranda of his single-storey yellow-coloured bungalow.

Percy had a German Shepherd, a huge emperor whose doe-eyed benevolence belied his fearful appearance. But Prince, as the beautiful Berlinesque thing was called, was friends with Charlie and Lucy. Prince was choosy about those he green lighted. Charlie would often flatter him: 'Why didn't Percy call you King?' Prince usually dismissed these infantile blandishments with royal insouciance, albeit the flattery didn't hurt. Thus, when Charlie accidentally shrieked in horror when a bat swooped low on him from the canopy-like trees above, Prince ran to see who the trespasser was but on seeing Charlie and Lucy there, he pretended as if he had seen nothing. But Percy hated intruders and looked suspiciously towards the source of the sound. Prince crouched low, covering both Lucy and Charlie from Percy's blurred line of vision. With a wink,

Prince left the lovers alone.

Feeling a wee bit nervous, Charlie and Lucy gingerly tiptoed away and finally found the secluded spot that they were looking for. It was in an unused garage whose door handles were corroded and its once heavy metal exterior had several cracks and holes. It creaked against the flurry of blustery breeze. Parked majestically in that dilapidated place was a piece of marvel: a grand old Impala car, a rare antiquity in the age of Kia. But for tonight that priceless artefact was converted into the ultimate lovers' sanctuary. The only eye witnesses to Charlie and Lucy's clandestine affair were the corpulent frogs who croaked as they jumped from one dirty puddle to another nearby, their large marble-like eyeballs nonplussed by the lovers above.

It was a balmy night and the stars shone bright on a cloudless sky. The moon itself was luminescent although it resembled a half-eaten apple that my mother would often find tossed in the dustbin after the kids' breakfast was over. Charlie leaned forward and gave Lucy a lick on her nose. 'You are so clumsy, Charlie boy.' 'Let me teach you how to kiss.' And then away from their homes where people were frantically searching for them, a few hundred metres away from where Percy Mistry snored wildly, amidst the sound of crickets, frogs and innumerable nocturnal insects, they made love. They say that we only copulate during seasonal heat, when we are biologically wired for a mate. But this felt different to the duo engaged in unbridled passion. Afterwards, they lay next to each other, looking up at the sky that seemed to have a darker tinge of blue.

'I love you,' said Charlie.

'I love you more,' replied Lucy with a big smile.

Humans take nine months to introduce another clamorous brat into the world, bawling and loud from day one. We take just nine weeks, once again showing more agility and alacrity on pressing matters. On 12 February, two days before Valentine's Day, Lucy gave birth to six miniature Dachshunds, each as large as a modern-day Chinese mobile phone. We all looked alike. Well, almost. One was different. It had a crooked tail. And that was me.

2

WE HAVE VISITORS

'Love is an irresistible desire to be irresistibly desired.'
—Robert Frost

Humans are born in one's, probably 99.99 per cent of the time. Duplicates (they give it the respectable title of twins) are rare. Triplets and quadruplets are like sighting asteroids maybe. Fact is they are no match to our reproductive capacity. No way,

Jose. We are serial manufacturers of puppies. We need no perfumed rubber and birth control measures; what's sexual intimacy with a protective film around the male thingy even if they have a strawberry flavour? Seriously, humans lack spontaneity. This foreplay, a pre-production investment seems like such a colossal waste of time. It is like washing a mango in detergent for an hour before peeling and eating the delicacy with whipped cream. We believe in PDA. We are the real romantics, uninhibited and fully expressive, no-holds-barred. We are perpetual hippies, not just a generational phenomenon like yours that disappeared with the Beatles.

My mother Lucy was an angel, valiantly moving around carrying several hyperactive bobbing things that made her stomach sag, scratching the floor. She also farted incessantly which was usually triggered by the pyrotechnics of her offspring in her tummy. Pregnancy is not easy on our breed, as we are quite Lilliputian to start with. And end with too, honestly. Lucy looked like a fried sausage on cholesterol steroids. And yet she glowed, her beatific smile never deserting her sweet face for a moment. Humans are either too circumspect or overbearing when it comes to childbirth, right? They read Dr Spock, do breathing exercises, crave for perpetual attention and eat endless dosas. Even the awkward husband joins in for the charade although he is not the one who will take the epidural injection. Moral support, it seems, although I believe it is to mollify the lady's irrepressible urge to break his jaw. That's why Charlie preferred to do the disappearing act, I think, when the crunch moment arrived.

Charlie, the ultimate personification of muscular machismo, like some political leaders, was basically lily-livered. He loved Lucy but could not bear to see her in pain. Thus when D-day arrived, and my mom knew that the turbulence within was rather unusually kinetic, Charlie chose to stay at his home, anxious, and worried as hell. He could always blame it on his master's instructions to stay indoors. The co-conspirator had sown his seeds, now Lucy would be left holding the baby. Babies actually. Our family maintained the operating average; there were six of us who tumbled out one after the other into Mumbai's terribly polluted environment, cacophonic street sounds and cramped space, watched by terrified-looking godparents who probably thought that my mother did not believe in full stops. Thankfully, she responded to their desperate prayers at some point. I am not aware of where I stood in the sequence given the limited space I had for manoeuvring out of the crowded exit door, but I almost slipped and hurt my head during that chaotic stampede.

We were a badly behaved bunch from day one. The ordeal over, Lucy looked proudly at her battalion, her munificent visage having an incandescent shine. As for the six of us, we just tumbled and fell with every step we took. Or every move we made. Or every breath we inhaled.

Charlie and Lucy had ensured gender equality; half of us were coy and cute, the other half was crude and curmudgeonly. As you must have guessed by now I belonged to the latter coterie. But it seemed weird to me that my godparents looked at me a wee bit longer with a palpably overawed look than the others. I often scratched my head (usually with my stronger left leg) to wonder why; I was cocksure I was by far the smartest dude around, but curiosity was killing the cat. Then one day I discovered why I was an object of such prodigious puzzlement—I was the only one among my exuberant siblings who was totally black. Jet-black, is how they described me. Not a strand or an iota of brown hair, which most of them had. I looked at myself in this giant rectangular mirror that almost kissed the ceiling and found a dashing, debonair hero staring back at me, my long nose sandwiched between two large ears flopping indifferently downwards. A pair of hazelnut-brown eyes gleamed boastfully. I liked the handsome stud with an expansive chest, like a dark-suited James Bond of mini-Dachshunds. Modesty is a good thing, but we should never be apologetic about what we are good at, whether acquired or inherited. My tail, curved upwards at the far end by a few centimetres was perhaps symbolic of my unique distinction. I was different. My legs were barely two and a half inches long but they were robust enough to support my long horizontal frame covered in a resplendent black texture. I overheard someone saying: 'He looks like a well-curated deep-fried black sausage.' Then they chuckled. Since I had no idea what they meant, I walked away from their silly merriment. I could never suffer bad jokes. Or trite conversations.

I remember I was also mama's favourite boy from the very beginning. She always cuddled me close at nights when the air conditioner made the room freeze, even as everyone protested and tried to elbow me out. I could be stubborn, you know. It was an epic battle, where the most coveted space was the circular curve of Lucy's tender tummy. Warm it felt, and we surrounded Lucy from all sides. Once we were all asleep, Lucy would gingerly extricate herself from the intractable bundle of mess, and then would have her food, or whatever remained of it. Exhausted, she would then catch a quick nap before we discovered that the elixir of our life was missing. My mother was the world's greatest mama, and if I could have caffeine like the humans, I would engrave that on my tea cup. But this interminable reverie of Lucy and all of us brothers and sisters had to end one day. It happened rather abruptly.

Approximately a few weeks after we were born, we were all suddenly huddled into a bunch, and were told to stop whining and behave ourselves. While it was conveyed with contrived congeniality, I was not fooled. I did not

like being told what to do. I stoutly refused. I concede my godparents had been basically very magnanimous, indulging us with unrestrained abundance. We were noisy, dirty, hard to control, and enjoyed being a nuisance. But after a few weeks of extravagant rowdiness, we were told to be better behaved. Too early for education, no? Then we were groomed too, as if we were graduating from a finishing school. They even made us wear a silly bow, get our bums brushed and respond to their guttural sounds by wagging our tail. 'Seriously?' I soon discovered why.

We saw several families coming to inspect us as if were aliens from outer space. The consistent factor among them was a sloppy father, a hyperventilating mother, and wild children. It was hard to say who was worse. We were happy as it was, messed up, pooping everywhere, wetting the floor and wrestling on it, watched by our indulgent sweet-faced Lucy. We were an exciting panoply of free love, but our blissful world would soon change. Lucy's seventh sense (humans are still stuck at sixth I was told) told her that there was something not right. In fact, there was something seriously wrong. We were soon to be separated.

I was angry. This was so unfair. I adopted an obdurate position. I refused to budge. I snuggled close to Lucy who appeared disconsolate at being torn apart from her still wobbly offspring (we walked as if we were inebriated, wavering from side to side). Five of us were ultimately showcased out in a line as if it was a beauty parade. Unknown to me, it indeed was. The humans had come to split our sweet family. 'Nasties!' And they can barely hold on to their own given their divorce rates, these con artists. I waited nervously for the charade to come to an end so that we could start our own circus. I could hear voices. Lucy wept uncontrollably. So did I.

'That one, no, not that one, the other one. That's right.' 'Is this one sick? There is no fire in his belly.' 'No, we don't want a she-dog. Too much problem maintaining them when they are on heat.' (Gender discrimination starts with the way we are adopted) We heard a smorgasbord of voices. They sounded enthusiastic all right but were also insufferably irritating. My godparents listened to a chorus of people speaking over each other and it was obvious that my poor brothers and sisters were being meticulously inspected by some peculiar strangers with awful listening skills. Lucy looked worried, cocking her ears at the door to make sense of what was going on. Were her babies safe? I consoled her by giving her a kiss and convinced her that our godparents would never allow any of us to be hurt. Ever. We sat side by side waiting for our family to be reunited. Outside, the commotion continued.

An hour or so later, the anarchy appeared to diminish. One could hear footsteps departing down the hallway. The door opened and my siblings ran back as swiftly as Usain Bolt, tripping over each right into Lucy's open arms. Their horrific nightmare was over. I was so thrilled to see them again after those traumatic few hours. But my happiness was transitory. There was only one of my sisters who would be left behind. And me. The rest were all scheduled to go away after a shampoo bath later that day. Our family stood defenestrated after some hard cash had changed hands. Four of my siblings would be taken away by those gremlins. My super-brat younger bro (he was smaller than me also) who had the naughtiest eyes imaginable, glinting perennially with curiosity, would go. We had barely gotten to know each other. There was a madness in our method that only we understood; it was beyond human comprehension. Humans want perfection over spontaneity, we prefer outrageousness over order. But love is like a torrential downpour that brooks no embankments. It must be allowed to find its own way. Feelings cannot be disciplined, you know. We Dachshunds live by that maxim.

That night I saw the doleful face of my little sister, who looked so vulnerable I held her tight and close, fully aware that we too would part at some point. It was inevitable. We had no control over our destiny. But tonight, was ours. We were together. And we had to live in the moment. Now. So we lay on top of each other in a bedraggled mess, encircling Lucy whose warmth was the only blanket we needed. We were determined never to let Lucy be alone. We would run away if we had to, dig a secret tunnel or something leading to Charlie's home. My elusive absent father who we knew was a brooding helpless wreck but could do nothing to keep his family intact. Lucy's sobs were muted but with my soft lick of her closed eyes I tried to mollify her. I love you, I told her. And for the first time that night, I think I saw a faint smile on her face.

3

MAMA MIA!

*'Never regret. If it's good, it's wonderful.
If it's bad, it's experience.'*
—Victoria Holt

The weeks following the big sale when four of my siblings had been transacted for were sublime in their serenity. Firstly, there were fewer curious deranged families turning up to see my sis and me, and secondly, Lucy had cheered up after her prolonged state of melancholy. The juvenile parade had ended. Thankfully. At least temporarily. Human behaviour is profusely complex; they encourage us to fornicate (it is a hugely profitable industry called 'breeders') so that we produce puppies and then separate us for monetary gain. It's an epitome of money-grubbing. It is a callous enterprise. True, we are supposed to be man's best friend (lucky you!) but would they sell off their own children to the highest bidder (I know some were forced to in South America until that fellow Lincoln tried to rescue them around the Civil War in the middle of the nineteenth century. Not surprisingly, these monsters assassinated the good man). I was chaffed with the hypocrisy of humans. Of course, in our case it was totally different; we were the kicking vestiges of the romantic rendezvous between the stud Charlie and the curvaceous Lucy. We were not part of the assembly-line cookie-cutter business model. Sadly, our godparents could not afford to keep us all. Not even one. Except Lucy, of course.

My sis and I kept enduring these exasperating oddballs who kept dropping by to check us out. I had a clear strategy to piss them off: I would actually pee on them. Then I would look at them with a I-dare-you-to-buy-me-now look. It worked to immaculate perfection. My sister was far too magnanimous to indulge in these sandbagging tactics and I feared that her congenial demeanour would prove costly. It did.

A strange couple walked in, with the man continuously on his mobile phone, talking about bulls and bears. I wondered why the jackass was not buying them instead of us mini-Dachshunds. His wife, who looked like a jewellery showroom on wheels, seemed as if she was out there to buy potatoes. 'Show me, show me, where are they?' she rattled as if she was on a steep treadmill running on full speed. Our godparents were dignified people who seemed quite annoyed at the egregious behaviour of these dorky people. Promptly, we were summoned. I was called first, as they wanted a boy (naturally, these sexist wimps). The diamond bandbox picked me up very gingerly and I was soon getting suffocated by this poisonous gas called Chanel. It was unbearable. 'Very cute boy, such a nice black boy, even if stinky,' she said, as she cuddled me in her rather sofa-size stomach. I remained unresponsive, unmoved by her friendly overtures. 'Khadoos-che,' said the man on the mobile phone, briefly interrupting his non-stop conversation about something called crypto. I gave him a dirty look, pregnant with contempt. I then proceeded to pee on the lady's exquisite saree that had some gold embroidery of some sort. It looked kitschy but expensive. It worked. 'Can we see the bitch, please?'

said the lady, angrily, hurriedly dropping me to the floor. I loved the landing on the slippery wet puddle I had created and promptly ran to Lucy who was watching my rehearsed performance with unconcealed joy. We chuckled. But now was my sister's turn. And she was a dead giveaway. Her eyes were angelic, her flawless features (her tail was normal) strikingly attractive. And she was a personification of sweetness too. The lady who seemed to be in a tearing hurry took to her like an Eskimo to cappuccino. But the man on the mobile phone appeared worried. 'Bitch-che.' At that point, the lady stomped her feet and threatened to leave him if he did not agree with her choice. I thought that would be the best thing to happen to humanity. Unfortunately, the jackass capitulated. Then I heard him argue vehemently with our godparents about a discount because of the 'bitch' factor. On being told to take the first flight out to Syria, he brought up inflation. That did not work either. Fuming and with great reluctance, he pulled out a chequebook, scribbled something on it, and then walked out in a huff. A few seconds later we heard the thud of a car door closing. The fashionista followed holding my sister close who seemed bewildered by what lay ahead of her. Lucy and I barely exchanged looks with her before she disappeared from our view. Within seconds she was gone. Forever.

Now there was one. Me. The only one left. Our small room suddenly felt like a giant warehouse. My mother became extremely possessive and protective about me. Maybe she feared the worst, about me being given away to a shelter kennel in case no one wanted me.

She had heard nasty stories about the way we were treated there. She thought her son deserved the best, the typical mother's sentiment quotient. She worried about her slightly arrogant fellow with an attitude and a tail that swerved  vertically upwards at the tip, like a hard iron hook. I was happy though. Perhaps I was destiny's child meant to be forever with my darling mother. The first pup to do so, our own Neil Armstrong taking a giant step for the dog brotherhood. But fate had other things in store.

It was a lazy summer afternoon around 3.30 p.m., when I heard the doorbell ring. Both Lucy and I woke up with a jerk from our afternoon siesta. We did not like the sound of that bell at all. It had a shrill staccato outburst which was seriously grating on our stretched nerves. But like everything else about humans we endured these shenanigans. We saw two people walk in and exchange polite greetings at the door with our godparents. Hmmm…that seemed a bit unusual. We were used to men-at-work business-as-usual types for whom we were nothing more than a garage sale. The visitors sat down. A lot of meaningless conversations continued. Perhaps they were just neighbours, I thought. Lucy and I prepared to happily snooze away the rest of the afternoon. But even as we turned back, my male godparent came at the door and said: 'Will you say a hello, little fellow?'

'Yes, of course,' I said to myself. I will pee on them also. Reluctantly, I ventured out, Lucy gingerly dropping me to the edge of the door.

I saw a reasonably tall bespectacled girl, peach-complexioned, with a nose turned awkwardly northwards, and when she smiled, she had a metallic formation of stainless steel protecting her teeth. But she had the kindest eyes I had seen among all the bat-shit crazy visitors. She appeared like a precocious teenager with a heart of gold. She was accompanied by a mid-sized modestly built gorilla who appeared to be suffering from a mid-life crisis. His curly hair was deliberately badly combed to conceal his fast-receding hairline, and his dishevelled beard needed some emergency housekeeping. His moustache seemed undecided on whether it needed to point upwards like my tail or be perpendicular to his sausage lips. That's why I thought he was a gorilla having a bad hair day. He seemed like he had ants doing a Lewis Hamilton race in his pants; he looked unusually energized, and could barely sit still. I thought he needed to take a tranquillizer. Most of them do.

The moment she saw me the toothy girl leapt with unbridled joy. Surprisingly, what seemed to have got her delirious was my unmissable crooked tail. She took me gingerly in her arms and gave me an endless hug and interminable kisses. Then she went dancing around the room with me, gently patting my back while my paws rested on her bony shoulders (clearly she needed some bad cholesterol). Everyone else watched her solo West End-kind spirited ballet performance mesmerized. I need to be honest here—there was something so genuinely warm about her compared to the others that I actually enjoyed that bumpy ride. Regretfully, she then handed me over to the man who was clearly her father although they could have been from Paris and Patna, that's how different they looked.

The gorilla held me so awkwardly my hind legs pained as they were getting crushed in his tight left-hand grip. He was admonished by Ms Toothy, his daughter: 'Dad, stop being idiotic. Hold him like this.' She demonstrated by forcing him to loosen his grip, while not dropping me off. He tried but failed miserably again. The gorilla was incorrigibly clumsy. A hopeless case. And in the absence of Ms Toothy, a serious risk factor. And yet I could not stop laughing at his comic fumbles. But when I looked at him closely, I saw nothing but love. Between the father-daughter duo, I saw a combination of Santa Claus and Tooth Fairy. It seemed as if he had been looking out for me for a while. His joy was so obvious. His adoration of my little compass-box frame was apparent. At that moment I took my split-second executive decision; if I had to live with these gawkish humans, I had rather be with this blundering oaf and his saccharine-sounding daughter. The gorilla was not a normal sort, but neither was I. And what's life without taking risks? Even the small snail only moves forward when it sticks its neck out, right? I left the gorilla stunned by licking his overgrown stubble. Ms Toothy rolled in laughter. So did my godparents. I was taken.

Extraordinarily, Lucy seemed delighted that I found crackpots who genuinely wanted me — warts, curve-tailed, burps and all. 'You know, my little son, I think they would have chosen you among all your brothers and sisters even if they had a choice. Be grateful for that always.' And I thought I had green lighted them! Both the gorilla and his daughter spent considerable time consoling Lucy, and that made my mother open her tear ducts. But with happiness. She was not fearful of me going to a dog shelter any more.

It was time to say goodbye after all. That dreaded ineluctable moment had arrived. My mama and I hugged each other and cried. And they all left us alone during those final moments.

Lucy came to the main door, standing beside my godparents as they circumspectly took me away. I looked back at her one last time, and in a flash my entire childhood played out as if in an amorphous reel. Goodbye mama!

I would never see her again.

4
HOME WITH WEIRDOS

'Human beings who are almost unique in having the ability to learn from the experience of others, are also remarkable for their apparent disinclination to do so.'
—Douglas Adams

I sat in this noisy contraption that was like an armoured vehicle, called a car. Clearly, this family was remarkably organized because I could see that they were prepared for me—there were wet wipes aplenty. Perhaps they were aware of my preternatural ability to pee at call. There was a light blue cushion with miniature puppy faces on them (looking very camera-friendly), although they were certainly not the debonair Dachshunds. They looked infinitely less distinguished and distinctive. Whatever, my posterior rested on them with insouciant ease. I felt comfortable. The young missus who I shall name Missy (to protect her right to privacy) could not contain her joy at cuddling me, frequently picking me up from my well-adjusted snuggle, and giving me an endearing look laced with solicitude. I took full advantage of her proximity and plonked myself on her lap as if it was my birth right. Missy reciprocated by squeezing me closer to her. Honestly, I was secretly thrilled. These humans were different from the other chumps I had seen earlier.

In the meantime, Missy's father was driving the car as if he had had gallons of frothy beer, his attention frequently diverted towards the little creature he was taking home. Missy hollered at him: 'Dad, you will kill us.' At which point, I felt a rude jerk followed by the sound of screeching tyres. If Missy had not been holding me tight, I would have flown straight away to the driver's seat. There was a momentary silence, followed by Missy's outburst.

'That was an irresponsible brake you took, Dad,' Missy continued to give her grizzly, undisciplined and bewildered-looking father a piece of her mind. He was good at suffering in silence I discovered.

Since it was my first day with the family it called for some smart masquerading on my part. I pretended as if I was not aware of the melodrama on the drive back. One must be non-judgemental as long as one can remain non-judgemental. The grizzly fellow who I will hereafter refer to as Beard, was on cloud nine and I could sense that he was valiantly and unsuccessfully trying to restrain his jumpy emotions. I could see he was smiling from ear to ear, mostly to himself, as Missy was clearly incommunicado. Thankfully Missy was there with me because if I had been alone with Beard, I would have certainly needed either a yoga treatment or a physiotherapist before I reached wherever they were taking me. For some strange reason, he kept hooking his finger into the curved part of my tail as if he could straighten it. Fool. But if he was just messing with me, he was doing a good job of it.

'How much did you pay for him?' asked Missy, and my ears cocked up, as I was curious to know my net worth. There is no free lunch with our pedigree types.

'Ten thousand bucks,' uttered Beard, sounding extremely proud that he could afford me.

Personally, I think a zero was missing somewhere. My godparents had demonstrated a charitable disposition for sure, because I was convinced I had a much higher brand valuation. Where can you find a jet-black mini-Dachshund with a twisted tail? I was a bonanza, a one-in-a-billion acquisition, like buying an Apple stock before the iPod hit the market. Anyway!

'Dad!' ordered Missy noticing Beard's bothersome twiddling of my tail. There was a sharp condemnation of his silliness, which forced him to hurriedly disengage with his peculiar fetish. I mentally prepared myself to be requiring my sharpest faculties to fix this weirdo. The moment came not too soon.

Missy reluctantly put me on Beard's lap as he was getting visibly restless that she had monopolized me. Driving safety, you clowns! On a no-choice basis I struggled to stand on his two skinny legs that were far from the bountiful mattress I was expecting. I looked at him making eyeball-to-eyeball contact with me which had him momentarily hypnotized. The crazy fellow was still driving, clearly a careless character. It was time to express my displeasure notwithstanding my earlier predisposition to be as civilized as I could be. So I quietly let loose my bladder that was in any case at bursting point. A deluge followed that spread quickly on to his blue denims giving them a hue of dark purple. Missy laughed like there was no tomorrow and I kept a straight face, expecting the benign monster to be really agitated with me. But to my complete amazement he did not seem to mind.

Not at all. On the contrary, he seemed overjoyed with what he thought was my child-like indulgence of him. 'Seriously? This was a red flag moment.' I knew then and there that my life was entering a zone of complete and unadulterated madness.

Humans are psycho, we knew. But this family was surely cuckoo. My fears would soon turn out to be right.

Beard rang the ding-dong doorbell, his enthusiasm getting the better of him, while Missy seemed in a desperate hurry to show me to the rest of the occupants behind a chocolate-brown door with an unpretentious traditional design. I heard someone from behind the door with a gruff voice exclaim in breathless anticipation: 'They are here! They are here!'

The door opened and I saw this plump girl, most unlike the bag of bones Missy was. She looked like she loved milk chocolates, potato fries and melted cheese on a bacon sandwich for breakfast. She had short hair which was not-so-neatly combed. She appeared like a sporty kind, who had little time for frivolous things like Barbie dolls. 'Is rugby her favourite obsession?' I wondered. There was a rugged toughness to her spirited personality. I figured early that she saw in me a doubles partner for tennis maybe. There was an indescribable sweetness about her though that was so apparent. Her face was a canvas of spontaneous feelings of love which was so welcoming to me, like that one small handkerchief you are looking for in a huge fashion store of esoteric monstrosities. The other person was tall, fair, much older, and had a no-nonsense air about her. Bro, she meant business, I told myself. She had a searching expression on her otherwise beautiful face, as if she was still in a dilemma whether to give me a rousing reception or treat me with calculated disinterestedness until she analysed the clear and present danger. But my sixth sense told me that the frozen glacier would melt when it encountered my manipulative eyes. It was in any case a mathematical impossibility for her to protest my presence—it was three against one. The triumph of democracy was at play.

I was put right in the middle of a large drawing room on the same moon-shaped light blue cushion adorned with obscure members of my canine species that had been carried upstairs from the car. A semicircle of faces now surrounded me. And they all looked at me in wonderment as if they could not believe what they were seeing. I probably looked like half of an A 4 page, a glistening black mass of hair, four tiny legs barely two inches long with long flappy ears that fell indolently on to the floor. My pointed nose resembled the now grounded Concorde jet that flew from Paris to New York in four hours flat. My nostrils, by the way, are sharp. My roasted coffee-bean-coloured eyes were on perpetual alert. Not to mention, my darned crooked tail, of course. A snapshot of the conversation that followed is given below:

Missy: 'He is so cute! He is sleeping with me tonight.'

The plump girl (I correctly assumed she was Missy's sister, and I shall hereafter refer to her as Mo): 'Oh my god! I have never seen anything like it! He looks like an overgrown rubber, no?'

The lady with a stern face that was beginning to show manifestations of an emerging crack, interjected: 'I wonder if it will remain at this size only. Anyone knows how big these mini-D's grow up to?'

Bearded man butted in: 'This is insane, man. But at least the house will now have a better hormonal balance.'

'That sounds so patriarchal, misogynistic and boomer-like,' said Missy and Mo in chorus as if they were part of Spice Girls once upon a time.

I listened to the inane absurdities with a straight face. These guys were really messed up; they all spoke at the same time but asked the other to shut up and listen to them when they spoke. Listening does not come to the human species easily, I can vouch for that. Talking nonsense does.

I thought of my mama Lucy all alone by herself and gave her a big warm hug in my mind, choking with emotions. I missed her. Terribly. But this was my new home. And despite  their rather jejune over-the-top ridiculous behaviour and uncontrolled hysteria at having me around, there was something genuinely very sweet about them. They could not hide their exhilaration at seeing a little black sausage. I preferred the extravagant craziness to the alternative: studied starchy tidiness. This was going to be my family now. I had promised myself I would reciprocate their warmth if they endeavoured to take the initiative. They had. So, I gingerly got up, looked at each one of them one by one, smiled and said: 'Thank you for having me.'

5

HI OLLY

*'If I had to live my life again,
I'd make the same mistakes, only sooner.'*
—Tallulah Bankhead

My arrival had led to unrestrained celebrations in the Family (I shall conceal their surname to prevent caste and religious polarization which is quite in vogue, I was warned by my mother). Everyone had a permanent grin; Missy and Mo were ecstatic, Big Mama seemed reconciled to her fate, and Beard, of course, needed no excuse for looking pleased with himself.

I was given a big bowl of milk with some glucose biscuits soaked in it. It was delicious and would become my go-to mood enhancer. I was just slurping gleefully away on it when I heard a low-key growl. I stopped, frozen with fear. 'What the hell was that? A dinosaur? A tiger?' Frightened up to my curved tail, I slowly turned towards where that rumbling sound had come from.

It was the first time I had seen anyone who looked like us (four legs and a tail) but who did not look exactly like us. He was far from being a fried red meat for sure. He was like a loaf of shaggy white bread. In the US of A, the white supremacists would probably lionize him. He resembled a round bundle of white fluffy wool, a lot of hair going everywhere. He was, surprisingly, not much bigger than me (thankfully); his wet nose was like a little black ball-bearing on a crumpled white sweater. I thought he was blind; his eyes were hidden in that hairy fuzz. But he could clearly see with 20/20 vision because as he marched towards me taking measured authoritative steps, I sensed with trepidation that he knew exactly what he was doing. The only consolation was that his tail was wagging vigorously concomitantly as if he had not seen anything as outlandish and outrageous as me either. Thus, he had no plans to eat me alive.

The nervous moments were broken by Missy and Mo.

'Black and white' went the girls in the family, especially Missy, the one with the braces and a falsetto voice. She even sang a tune that I would later know was crooned by a guy with feet sharper in its locomotion than ours, a certain Mr Jackson.

Mr White (I didn't know his name yet) came close to sniffing distance. We looked at each other, eyeball to eyeball, even as the Family clearly stiffened in anticipation of a skirmish  of sorts between two toothless wonders, although they pretended to be watching a friendly circus. To an outsider it would be like we were daggers drawn, two underdeveloped fools acting ultra-masculine before a dogfight. But when I looked longer and deeply into his eyes all I could see was pure unfiltered love. Behind that deliberate Drama Queen histrionics for high impact, Mr White appeared to be like just one big sentimental fool. He could barely hide the fact that he was thrilled to see another creature that came closest to him, even if the trespasser was black enough to camouflage in the dark. Evidently, the Family had already got on his nerves.

Mr White circled me like Kung-fu fighters do, spending a lot of time inspecting my posterior (the rogue!) before he gently trooped away, dismissing me like a third unwanted shoe. I was not worthy of any further investment of his time, at least for the moment. This was followed by something peculiar. He walked on top of a neatly spread-out newspaper which was pink in colour and whose headline was about bulls and bears having a field day in turns, which apparently enabled these humans to make a lot of money. But Mr White had visible contempt for such larceny; he stood there and without lifting his legs he peed for a good fifty-two seconds on that big bold text with a graphic image zigzagging upwards with smiley faces. 'The price of education,' I told myself. I also realized that I had triggered emotions in Mr White that he found profoundly moving. 'Good for him... And for me.'

While everyone roared in laughter at Mr White's generous sprinkling, Big Mama was not amused. She had a peach-coloured complexion which flushed beetroot red when something did not agree with her, and most things did not. Her aristocratic nose then turned further skywards, which only made me stretch my head to a 90-degree angle to catch her face. 'Ouch!' She had large marble eyes atop sharp features that incorporated semi-high cheekbones and a distinctive chin. It was evident that the unkempt Beard must have been burning the candle at both ends to have captivated her. She looked like a tough nut to crack behind her otherwise charming carriage.

'Please stop that flood from trickling on to the carpet before it gets ruined,' she instructed the two girls. They in turn passed on that instruction to two other young girls who were vigorously texting away on their mobile phones in the kitchen and pretended not to hear them.

But a shrill tornado that emanated from Big Mama shook them out of their act. There was a dramatic uptick in household energy; order was established immediately after that loud bellow. The Family clearly practised  empowerment with passion. I had barely been in this large house (it was bigger than the cribbed, cabined and caged place I had lived in earlier with my family) for an hour, and I could sense that its principal occupants were clearly neurotic. No two people agreed with each other, and they spoke through some supernatural synchronicity at the same time. I suspected they were simultaneous announcers of flight operations at airports. My gentle eardrums were reverberating. I think Mr White felt it too, and he therefore gave me a sly wink that said 'Welcome, bro, now you are screwed too'.

The next day I was being carried all over the place and introduced to the various rooms in the house as if they were real estate agents desperate to negotiate a good bargain. The kitchen smelt good — 'Did I sniff chicken stew?' The Family was clearly trying to impress me. Mr White followed the procession from one room to the other, always keeping a watchful guard over me in case the Family did something scandalous, like inadvertently put me in the washing machine (I am black, remember?) for instance. Such calamities were fortunately avoided. And I must admit reluctantly that although the Family was quite a challenging proposition, they were genuinely over the moon at having Mr White and me around them. There was a reason.

In every room that I was transported to there was a stunning photograph of a big beast with the most charismatic aura that I had ever seen; his face was twice my current body size, and his mane was that of a Lion King (yes, that same lord of the jungle who can sing). It had regal imperiousness written all over it, like he was adorned in an emperor's attire. His ears, unlike mine (which drooped downwards) stood at nearly 90 degrees in geometric perfection. His mouth was open in a big wide pant, his salami tongue hanging out giving him the look of the ultimate reliable bodyguard. He was. I overheard that he was a German Shepherd whom the Family had given a stylish name that no dog had been called before (or since, I guess) — Amadeus, named after an Austrian musical genius allegedly. Amadeus had been the Family's first connection with the species superior to them (can you hear me chuckling?). They were devastated when he died after suffering from the

aftermath of a heatstroke. He had been their project of compassionate indulgence for thirteen years. Within a few weeks, Mr White, a Lhasa Apso from the disputed land of the holy Dalai Lama appeared in their lives to fill the enormous vacuum left behind by Amadeus. The fact is that Mr White was like that elusive catharsis they frantically sought.

After a while everything was hunky-dory although Amadeus was indeed a legend. Mr White had brought cheer to a despondent home. Then how did I join the party? There is a story there too.

It seems that Beard was once running at the Race Course (a place for horses, but what can you do with a man's incorrigible vanity, folks?) to lower his LDL cholesterol (it seems butter chicken was to blame) and increase his depleting testosterone levels when he first saw an extraordinary replica of me. He got so carried away  by one of my older cousin's ding-dong walking style that he promptly fell in love with mini-Ds. Characteristically he chased the young shapely girl with an hourglass figure who had our cousin on a pink polka-dotted coloured leash with Paris Hilton ensconced in those circles. She wore headphones that played acid rock. How do I know that? Because she never heard Beard's several entreaties as she energetically bobbed her head up and down with Beard waving his hand to attract her attention. Eventually, Beard literally stopped her in her tracks by standing menacingly in front of her, leading to raised eyebrows from several geriatric types who almost reached for the police helpline.

The supermodel, who was unruffled by the sudden appearance of a chimpanzee obstructing her rapid march, told Beard that the little thing barely visible from that height was a mini-Dachshund. 'Miniiiiieeeeee Dasssshund,' he went, mispronouncing our breed as most ignoramuses do. He then went home, hook, line and sinker in love with our distinguished breed. He had made up his mind to get one. And so here I was, Beard's favourite obsession, following a measly 10,000 bucks of investment.

Mr White was not a good actor, I surmised. While he was pretending to enthusiastically follow me around, he seemed a bit miffed as well that his monopoly was now under threat. He protested by letting out a few loud farts that had everyone scurrying for cover. He used that brief hiatus to give me a look that said 'Always remember two things; I am the big boss here, and your fart is a weapon of mass dislocation'. I acknowledged that by nodding my head and letting out an inaudible, dignified one myself. Behind his crooked teeth in a face that was covered with unkempt, uncombed, unhinged hair (like Beard, I would say), I could see the emergence of a wicked smile. But I still did not know his name.

'Oliver,' I heard the bespectacled buck tooth call; Missy I mean. Promptly, like a good obedient boy Mr White responded by wagging his small tail that curled upwards (unlike mine which was horizontal and was only twisted at the end) and stood in front of her, looking up for what appeared to be some goodies.

'Olly,' said her sister Mo. Mr White immediately turned leftwards and sat in front of her. Hmmm...this was very interesting. So Mr White had two names. Wow. He must indeed be very special. But Mr White was one of a kind. He even had a third name.

'O,' called Big Mama who had lightened up a bit by now. Mr White responded to that too, the crazy schizophrenic. It seemed rather bizarre that he was so phonetically versatile.

Much later after the Family seemed distracted with their mobile phones, Oliver and I at last got some time together. We both heaved a sigh of relief. We sat next to each other, our skins touching, two dogs from two different worlds, one of a German descent and a natural predator, the other, a spiritual if temperamental fellow from the land of Tibetan monks. We looked at one another and smiled. We would need to collaborate intelligently to survive this hyper-intense family; bonding was necessary. But we had each other. Olly would soon become my big brother. And unknown to me then I had also found my soulmate.

6

THOSE HEADY EARLY DAYS

'You are remembered for the rules you break.'
—Douglas MacArthur

Human beings are so lackadaisically discriminatory; they want a big double bed with a foamy mattress curated by orthopaedic designers to balance their heads at a 175-degree angle, supported by large pillows and cuddle-inducing blankets for themselves, while we are expected to sit on a pathetic apology of a quasi-rug with some discounted cotton wool packed in to deceive us. Olly being Olly was of course easily mollified but me being me I was not. This was blatantly unfair. As it is both of us were so minuscule in size, we could have been accommodated in a tenth of Beard and Big Mama's oversized bed. Clearly two's company and four's a crowd. But I made my discomfort palpable, looking up at Big Mama and Beard with a wistful expression, gently but persistently whining. Protests must gradually rise to a crescendo, that's part of strategic negotiations, which some right-wingers call a toolkit. Olly joined me too in this plaintive remonstrance. But that was still like water off a duck's back. Nothing seemed to work. But why?

I think the problem was Big Mama; she appeared to be a fastidious type, wanting everything to be spick and span, and would have little sufferance for deviations from her operating plans. Beard was more like us, and I could frequently hear Big Mama lambasting him for making the bathroom wet (but wasn't that the sole purpose of that malodorous room?) and dislodging the pillow by shifting it 12 degrees more to the right than to the left. It was nerve-racking even for a distant observer. Something told me Beard needed a therapist, and fast. Big Mama wore the pants, suit and the boot in the house for sure, and Olly and I soon realized that we would have to quickly master the art of political management for peaceful coexistence of us all. Keeping Big Mama happy and unruffled was crucial to our happiness model. Beard was an innocuous cipher, like an alliance partner in politics you could do without because you already had a majority. Like a fifth wheel basically, surplus and superfluous. But despite our heartfelt pleas, Big Mama did not seem to relent. It was time to target Missy and Mo. They appeared more malleable for sure, by comparison. In fact, they would be delighted to be co-conspirators in this back-door operation. But like in tennis and love life, timing was the key. It was my naming ceremony that did the trick.

The Family sat in a huddle in the drawing room as if it was a G-4 summit or something. Promptly several bizarre names were tossed around. In keeping with Big Mama's disciplinarian ways, the deadline to name me was restricted to four and a half days after my arrival at their doorstep. In keeping with the trend of urban pretentiousness of coming up with unusual, atypical names for their kids, a few esoteric ones were being tossed around for me as well. 'D-DeVito. Dishoom. Mini123 (it sounded a bit effeminate, I thought, and also more like a computer password). Black (one of the four was clearly a racist). Small. Ronaldo (what kind of a name was that?). Kale West.' There were several such inanities uttered and the author of each believed that they had the best name for me. Olly and I just sat there watching them engage in an acrimonious free-for-all debate with each trashing the other's choice instead of batting for their own. It was like watching 'The Nation Wants to Know' TV debate. Ultimately Mama came up with a brainwave: 'If we don't agree to my recommendation, you are all free to call him by your personal choices. He will be the first dog in the world to have four names.' Democracy had been summarily redefined. That's how I came to be called Louis. It was Big Mama's diktat. Everyone obediently nodded their heads as if that name had crossed their minds as well. Of course, as expected that name would undergo several iterations in the years ahead.

But now, back to the bed conundrum. To get your way with the human species, either you have to genuinely enjoy their overbearing indulgence, or you have to put on a great show of deference. I did the latter as Olly was the what- you-see-is-what-you-get types. He was a transparent dude, like one of those devout jholawalla's running a charitable trust for liberal values. I was politically more astute. I knew that to find a permanent abode on that huge comfortable bed I had to be a good boy, ignoring no one, making everyone feel special, and recognizing publicly that Big Mama was of course the first among equals. My artifice soon began to work. Mama, I gathered from some Sherlock Holmes-style eavesdropping, had been reluctant to get another dog into the house (Olly had chewed her shoes bought in a New York mall, and her Kashmiri carpet had taken more than its share of scrubbing in the town's most expensive laundry). Thus, it is she who had to be cajoled and captivated. So I put on my charm offensive. I followed Mama all over the house all day, and when she looked at me I looked back at her, trying to look as lachrymose as possible. She was a mother after all, and I had to invoke the sentiment in her that now I saw my four-legged, thick-tailed Lucy mama only in her. She had to see me as her sweet highly vulnerable little boy who could do with some serious appeasement. I persevered with this project with unflagging determination. It took time, but I went after my gameplan with the relentlessness of one Mr Cruise — mission impossible. It worked, even though it took a tad longer at nearly one year of sleeping on that horrible bed, where my only consolation was that Olly was nearby.

One night as I sauntered off dejectedly towards my bed on the far-right corner of the master bedroom with an Amazonian sulk, Big Mama came up to me and said: 'Baby, you are not sleeping alone any more. So stop making a long face.' She hugged me close, and you won't believe it, the warmth she radiated actually reminded me of my mother who I had not seen for so long. I nodded in appreciation, my tail involuntarily giving away my ecstasy. That night I slept like never before in my life since leaving Lucy's side, despite Beard's intermittent snoring that reminded me of the sounds of the exasperating SUVs I heard during the day.

The bed was warm and soft, like a lullaby song, and as I snuggled close to my new mother, I never wanted to be away from her ever again.

Olly was a moody fellow, his mood swings reminiscent of the form of cricketer Sachin Tendulkar before his retirement; it was both very good and very bad. It was speculated that he had a bit of the mercurial maverick, the Tibetan Terrier, in him. Ol (that's what I used to call him) was a sweetheart but he needed to be handled with kid gloves. Beard was so awkward with him we used to both laugh at his ham-handed approach. Big Mama though was a natural parent, a fine blend of genteel motherly forbearance and a school teacher's despotic ways. But after handling crazies like Missy and Mo you could probably handle anything, anyway, including a hungry crocodile. But even Big Mama had to create a huge melodramatic script when she had to trick Olly into taking a bath. 'Bath! Don't humans know that we are not meant to take baths? Ever?' Anyway, every dog has his day, I guess.

Now Mr Snow White loved running wild in the mud when it rained, his little paws soon looking like dark chocolate cupcakes. We would often be the only users of the building's sprawling garden, with most humans running on a treadmill, sweating immensely

THOSE HEADY EARLY DAYS

but effectively going nowhere. Because of my glowing dark complexion, I could easily camouflage in the dirt. Olly could not. In monsoons, Olly frequently looked a picture of mischief, his lovely fur interspersed with gooey mud, his face like that of Mowgli from *The Jungle Book*, a kaleidoscopic range of emotions ranging from 'Hey, I am a dude' to 'Sorry, I messed up'. Mama being a perfectionist was not in any mood to entertain his dirty shenanigans. All it took was a chewy and 'Olly is such a good boy' routine and Ol was hooked. Trapped. And arrested. Before long, I could see him getting sponged and soaped inside as he stood their wet and grumpy as hell, his face reminding me of a famous politician in India while giving a TV interview. But unlike that hot head, Olly could not just stomp off like that. My turn came soon after. And they did not even have to give me a delicious bone as a hook because unlike Ol, I could not even pretend to be angry. I was easy meat.

All through my life I have never comprehended (by now you know that many things about these people leave me flummoxed) why these humans take a bath daily, sometimes twice, when we never needed it, barring exigent situations like some mud-wrestling and gutter-walking. Clearly, they were dirtier, sweatier and had poor hygiene habits. Although Ol was exactly my size, unlike him, I was often impertinently bathed in a big oval-shaped basin. I thought that was body-shaming but other than a desperate resistance to it I could do nothing. Of course, the Family thought that was 'so cute'. They loved an easy conquer. The soap bubbles tasted awful and once I even choked on that repugnant detergent, which bought me a temporary reprieve (for two months I was spared the washbasin rinse). At once, everyone crowded around me, anxiously blaming each other for their reckless adventurism. I liked that. I liked attention. And I knew how to get it.

One evening, several moons later, the Family called out 'Louis-Olly' even as we were still rubbing sleep off our eyes. We were a twosome, inseparable, like joined at the hip; we were therefore always called in tandem. As we ambled into the giant drawing room, the Family stood there with big happy smiles on their faces. We were surprised by their enthusiasm at an unearthly hour of 8.30 a.m. in the morning. The tranquillity barely lasted a few seconds as a collective hoarse chorus took over: 'Happy birthday to you, happy birthday to you, happy birthday dearest Lou, L, Luke, Loocha (all four were used), happy birthday to you.' What followed was pure madness. They all picked me up in turns, smothering me with hugs and kisses, and making me roll on my back on their laps as they tickled me in places I could not access. I felt on top of the world. It was my first birthday. And the crazy manic family loved me with wild abandon. I kissed them back too. Both Missy and Mo actually wanted me to lick

their faces. I obliged. A clueless Ol also barked along.

Afterwards, Ol and I were treated to scrumptious mawa cakes from a nearby Parsi bakery. That would become our annual birthday tradition in the years ahead. Life was indeed a party.

7

THE MADNESS CONTINUES

'When I am good I am very good,
but when I am bad, I am better.'
—Mae West

When we were little kids (Olly was anyway just about six months older to me) all the Family fed us was fresh buffalo or cow milk (although I am an aficionado of fine-dining, I never knew the difference). I guess it was an attempt at assuaging their guilty conscience as they knew we missed our mother's nipples. Breastfeeding is breastfeeding. What's sauce for the goose is sauce for the gander, right? In any case, we barely had teeth so this overdose of milk was perhaps justified. We sincerely lapped it up.

But teething troubles surfaced soon enough. While I had the bark, Olly had the bite. The deceptively congenial-looking Lhasa Apso was a revelation. Ol's teeth from inception had deadly incisiveness. He was like Spielberg's Tyrannosaurus Rex.

Big Mama gave us both a big dressing down one day for having redesigned her Elizabeth Arden stilettos by changing the height of one shoe and removing a bit of red leather from another to create a zigzag innovative look that even Louis (copycat) Vuitton would not have contemplated. It clearly did not meet Big Mama's more fashionable expectations. She hollered at us while we sat dutifully with our heads bowed down. Olly was a brilliant at feigning innocence and I would dutifully co-share responsibility for his misdemeanours, which included not just shoes, but table legs, Missy's stuffed toys, Beard's socks, unread *Economic Times*, Mo's school textbooks, coasters, food tray (I am abbreviating this list because the publisher of this book might object). I never ratted on Ol and he would often lick my nose to express his gratitude. But back to the thorny issue, food.

Ol and I had a catastrophic problem ahead; the Family was vegetarian. Doomsday beckoned. By that I mean Big Mama (who as you might have guessed by now was the unofficial boss of the household) only ate greens and stuff — spinach, gourd, peas, potatoes, etc. Meat was taboo on account of some religious proscription. 'Weird,' I thought, 'we animals are genuinely secular.' We may look different and belong to variegated breeds, but our eating habits, customs and gastronomic predilections are common. Laissez-faire, no vigilantism is needed to check on our food habits. Our constitution is solid (pun intended). Everything works; we have a versatile palate. Humans may look the same or similar but they have created some insurmountable man-made walls between themselves. Caste, religion, gender, colour, creed, language, it is a long list. I don't think they know what collegial means. Their bad, as they say. Despite her steadfast adherence to age-old rituals, Big Mama had to make concessions to us. Here is why.

Thanks to divine intervention, Beard and the two delightful daughters loved meat. While they were not  permitted by the household operating manual to have it on the grand table where meals were customarily served, they could consume the meaty delicacies in the packets in which they were delivered. The regular culinary dishes were prohibited for use; the environment-unfriendly plastic was acceptable though. There was another caveat: food had to be eaten in the balcony, so that its putrefied aroma did not waft into the main kitchen to merge with some sattvik concoction.

Ol had olfactory senses that were extra-terrestrial. His nostrils could detect meat a few hundred miles away. So we had foreknowledge of when Missy had ordered a pepperoni pizza or Mo was likely to devour a juicy chicken burger layered with French fries and mayonnaise. Beard had a fetish for Punjabi butter chicken that floated alongside some creamy cholesterol. Honestly, it was really embarrassing to see such an old guy drool like a greedy kid would do for a raspberry lollipop. He was an embarrassing, gluttonous sort. But we were not complaining; the more the merrier.

Now all three of them would religiously share their meat with the two of us, mostly equitably, although Olly got a slightly bigger share being the elder. Fair enough.

Missy was a wee bit stingy about sharing her pork, which was a tad disappointing, because red meat is tantalizing. Mo was unpredictable; but when she did share, she gave us a disproportionately large share. Beard was magnanimous with most meats excepting mutton pepper fry. When no one was watching he  would drop big chunks surreptitiously on the floor, and although I could be faster than Olly, I chose to concede defeat because this is one time Olly could be a pain in the ass. He would give me a hollow threat. I am a peacenik, so I would choose to let him conquer the meat. But then these good fortunes smiled intermittently, mostly over the weekends only. For the most part, we were subjected to some wheat bread soaked in milk or rice with green vegetables, as if we were suffering from diabetes. Or needed an Ayurvedic detoxification. It was then that Olly and I discovered the Mahatma's famous satyagraha strategy. We went on fasts. There were days we just refused to eat cottage cheese and boiled rice. It was not easy, but protest we had to. Non-violent, of course. At a time when the country was celebrating a fellow called Godse, we were going Gandhian.

Our fast-unto-dinner revolt had the desired effect. It led to some intense debates on the dining table and eventually Mama lost overwhelmingly by 1-3. Unlike Putin, she conceded. While fresh meat remained prohibited, packaged dog food that came in shiny yellow plastic coverings was introduced. It was like manna from heaven. Chicken, lamb, beef, fish, the works, came in different curries, sometimes wrapped round a chewy. Our appetites whetted, we gorged. Incidentally, we guys can eat any time. Like we can sleep any time too (and we don't need sleeping pills). By contrast, humans need some deprogramming; just because they have a monotonous routine of breakfast, lunch and dinner, we were put in the same boring regimented process. It was awful. The schedule was like being in a concentration camp. Worse, consumption was slotted into a democratic structure: Olly and I were expected to eat from the same bowl, one after the other. Thanks to my Himalayan proportions (sarcasm is deliberate), Olly always started first. I always dreaded that if O loved that day's offering, I would quietly starve. But O was consistently considerate towards me. Or maybe he was watching his weight just like the Family was.

Humans are ridiculous. Some take their weight practically every day, sometimes without wearing a contact lens to feel slimmer, and they have the audacity to body-shame us. Can they do the dog pose which they call Adho Mukha Svanasana? Can they? We do it effortlessly whenever we want to. Without panting. Or complaining of a backache. We don't need no hot yoga and all that. 'Hypocrites, I tell you.' And yet the Family insisted that we must exercise regularly. Could they not see Olly and I race each other all over the house, slipping on the marble floor that was certainly not good for our small ankles, but which provided great entertainment to all and sundry? Frankly, what happened next got Olly and me really agitated.

In the early years, the Family's spoil-us benchmark was skyrocketing. The Family would frequently play with us downstairs in a rectangular-shaped garden that was only intermittently frequented by those constantly bawling babies that humans reproduce at regular intervals. Sorry for the digression, but they should learn  adaptation from us; we adjust to any situation with panache. These howling kids have their mamas hovering all around them; maybe that's why they cry so much. Anyway, so Olly and I chased balls, often getting into a competitive tussle at the end. The joke was that Missy would get so tired throwing the balls at us because we were indefatigable that she needed a sugary drink afterwards. Olly was a disciplined fetch fellow; he would dutifully get the ball back. I was just the opposite; does the winner ever return his trophy? Once I captured the ball, it was my property. Everyone thought I was a spoilt sport, but I was only adhering to the rules of the game. We were never tired of running and rolling on the green grass where we also sometimes found delectable stuff, like...a dead mouse, allegedly poisoned by the paranoid humans. And they keep saying live and let live! But then they also lynch their own to death, don't they?

In my opinion, Olly's most spectacular achievement was that he captivated Beard's poker-faced mother-in-law, famous for being particularly fastidious with a capital F. Needless to add, but Big Mama's expression conveyed enough sarcasm insinuating that Beard could possibly educate himself from Olly's charming manners. Even if he tried, I thought he would fall awfully short; Olly's soulful innocence was unparalleled, and his eyes had a magical humanity about them. TV channel cameramen did not quite think so, as Olly would stubbornly guard Beard, keeping a watch on them with a permanent gaze, sitting in a corner with a barely audible growl, while he talked rubbish to impress the world. I believe he barely got enough votes.

After the initial flush of delirious enthusiasm at having us both around, the law of diminishing something kicked in, I think. Although love was in abundant supply, the enthusiasm of the Family waned somewhat. Soon, the garden games began to dry up, the occasional walks stopped, and even the mad chase for the balls in the house became kind of sporadic. Olly and I would often wonder why humans take life so seriously. They are always chasing mirages; they are rarely satisfied with what they have. 'Don't they say success is getting what you want, happiness is wanting what you get?' Frankly, do they even read the self-help books they purchase at hefty discounts at book sales? Evidently not. So before I forget, why were Olly and I up in arms? Because the Family in keeping with the trend of delegation (which is a more sophisticated term for relinquishment) hired a dog walker. To make matters worse, his name was Bhola.

Bhola took his job seriously, which means he refused to smile. Firstly, why was he coming at such an unearthly hour, when it was hard to say whether it was morning or night? While I made peace with this ridiculous arrangement, Olly protested as only he could. He bit Bhola on his left hand, drawing some tomato ketchup in the process. Mama gave O a piece of her mind minus the intellectual copyright even as Missy and Mo giggled. I kept a straight face which given my pointed nose was a trifle easy, but I was thrilled too. In Mumbai, walking on the pavement is like traversing craters on the moon. They are uneven, broken, and disintegrating and can easily give you a slipped disc, unless you have fallen into a manhole earlier. Bhola came precariously close to falling in them but our prayers were unfortunately not answered. Initially, Bhola walked with amazing ferocity and I wondered whether he was walking us or working on his own fitness regimen given his protruding waistline. We were struggling to keep pace. But it proved to be a mere aberration and soon he was lumbering along, because of a new, attractive diversion. Bhola had started slowing down to flirt with the house help from the third floor of the fourth building next to our home. In fact, I thought we were all walking in circles around that house like a security force. I thought she dismissed his overtures just like I ignored the gadflies buzzing around my nose. But the new pace of walking suited us all.

Gradually the size of the walking tribe increased. Soon we were Gabby, Dumbo, Hoo, Ginger, Ol and me, six of us with the still indivisible Bhola. From the hushed whispers of jealous security guards in the building it seemed that Bhola had struck a goldmine because of the lazy owners and would soon buy himself a Porsche car. I usually led the pack during our walking expeditions as I was the fastest and unlike the big hulks who wanted to pee on every lamp post and shit on every cracked tile on the pavement, I had better bladder control. In all fairness while Bhola could not be blamed for failing to synchronize the pee and poo timings of six of us with varying bowel movements, he could have done much better. Hoo had a particularly odd habit of circling Ginger's shit seven times (as if he was solemnizing a marriage ceremony) before he would contemptuously drop a few sausages and look for another spot. All of us would wait patiently for this farce to play out every alternate day. Bhola stopped any pretensions of patience and would start walking us even as Hoo was halfway between a fart and a poo. Unlike others, I had already pre-selected my favourite place for my daily constitutionals; my home. On my chosen newspaper, *Bombay Times*.

Every day when we returned from the long exhausting walk, Olly and I would walk to the newspaper centrespread and shower the faces of the city's hottest supermodels. Mama was extremely unimpressed by our

charlatan conduct. 'We are paying a bomb to Bhola to make them crap outside and these guys come home and do their stuff. They have no sense of toilet-training.' She was right. And wrong. She was right about compensating Bhola a big fortune for confabulating with pretty house helps. But she was completely wrong about our toilet-training. We are told to answer nature's call at the first signs of discomfort. And yet we had controlled our urges because Bhola was an impatient rogue. Some humans we figured actually postpone their pee, for a variety of reasons, including the absence of clean tissues, wet floors, and sometimes traces of turd on the pot. How silly! And by the way, we are not the only ones who indulge in a pee war. I have overheard that grown up men like Beard shoot a fountain towards the ceiling to dwarf the previous guy's accomplishments. The size of the male ego. Seriously. So why blame us? Isn't imitation the best form of flattery?

The one thing both Olly and me dreaded was this short, scrawny, bespectacled old man with a grave countenance and stiff mannerisms, who seemed a perfect trailer of apocalyptic doom. He always wore a white open gown that flirted with his knees. He was always surrounded

by two equally unsmiling faces, who looked like his faithful acolytes, loyal accomplices to crime. Dr Rustam Vachcha was a terrifying prospect who we had to suffer at least once a year for some vaccines (I wish I could do a Djokovic). Did we have to? I hated that cold steel bed without any cushioning where we were pinned down, while Vachcha took out a dangerous-looking needle. I would look at Mama for help but for some strange reason she was totally disinterested in my predicament. In fact, I felt she was an accessory in this diabolical experiment. The two dull-faced assistants would hold my hands and legs, pressing them down with unwarranted force. These humans are such cheap bullies, two big burly men against one mini-D. This is called asymmetrical warfare, like Norway playing nuke games with North Korea. Then without even a flicker of empathy for me, Vachcha would prick the needle into my buttock. I hated that initial poke, it really hurt. Fortunately, the ordeal was short-lived, although the whole process was an excruciating torture. My friend Ol though was a different proposition. He would refuse to take things lying down. Olly had sharp teeth that would have made the Great White Shark blush with embarrassment. Doctor Vachcha though it seemed was prepared for his roar. And bite. That is the first time I saw this thing called a muzzle. But then wasn't that meant for human bloodsuckers, like this guy Hector Hannibal?

Why was Olly, the sweetest soul on this half of the Equator, being subjected to this horrendous thingamajig? Olly refused to be cowed down, and despite the muzzle, I could sense the trepidation in the blank-faced Mistry. He was not amused. Veterinary doctors must learn to smile more often, we surmised. And our parents could at least pretend to be less enthusiastic about taking us there.

Strange as it may sound there was still this one time when we would have preferred Dr Vachcha's nasty injections to being at home. And that was during a time when everyone went ballistic and started bursting bombs and polluting the poisonous air further. You know what I am talking about, right?

Why is making noise a form of celebration that the gods love (forget the putrid pollution for a bit)? We disliked Diwali from the bottom of our hearts, which would shrink like a violet under duress when the noise became insufferable. This is not to offend the majoritarian sentiment or anything, just honest feedback. Humans are bad enough for most of the year, cacophonous as hell. Why berate yourself further?

The Family was used to barking orders, all of them, but it was only Big Mama who really commanded respect from the house helps. There were two of them. They looked like twins, who walked around like robots on a premeditated mission. Beard was often ignored by them; they knew the food chain well. It was hard to comprehend why the Family could not walk to the kitchen and tell the cook that they wanted more milk in their tea or less sugar in the milkshake. Instead, they would shout from one end of the house, which invariably the cook never heard because she was busy talking to her boyfriend on the mobile phone, or because the pressure cooker was announcing its arrival at the central terminus.

When Diwali came, the Family dramatically went into silent meditation. Then the neighbours took over. As did the society. And the city itself became like an armaments factory, exploding rockets, interminable crackers, and flowerpots in a cornucopia of lights and noise. The latter killed our delicate eardrums. Olly and I were both frightened by this alien invasion that we later discovered was going to be an annual laceration. The Family itself was surprisingly well behaved and we were given post-dinner desserts by all of them when the other was not looking. I loved those little laddoos, syrupy sweet and succulent, they would melt in my mouth. They would also tell each other with concern written all over their faces that sugar was not good for canine metabolism. Frauds, just massaging their guilt pangs. All of them were consummate performers. But I loved them. They loved us like nuts and kaju barfi; despite their crazy antics, acrimonious fusillades and over-the-top energy, they were the best family I could have asked for. Olly too felt the same albeit he wished they were less unstable. Thus, for the two of us the toughest period of the year was the summers when the Family deserted us in an organized conspiracy.

One fine day after Missy and Mo returned from school, they looked ecstatic as they tossed their school

bag like a Frisbee from one end of the room to the other. We joined in the mayhem by aping them and running from one end of the house to
the other in between tripping the house help who almost crash landed on to the walls. There was much buoyancy in the air, as we got tossed around by them, tickled till we could not handle it any longer, and generally crushed under their body weight as they treated us like stuffed toys. But I also noticed that they were looking sorrowfully at us afterwards and talking in whispers out of our earshot, which made no sense amidst the mirth. Why were they so two-faced, happy and sad at the same time? But came evening time and the puzzle stood resolved. Out of several closets, big black suitcases emerged and Big Mama marshalled her leadership resources to decide what would go where; clothes, toiletries, shoes, cosmetics, medicines, cameras, shoes, etc. Everyone quietly obeyed. Beard's attempt at getting a word in was to no avail, he was contumaciously overruled. Mama had a checklist that travelled from her bedroom to the treadmill and she had to tick them all before the suitcases were officially cleared for transport. Beard kept tossing his underwear, shirts, caps, jeans, toothpaste and sundry items into his bag in no particular order, clearly revelling in the disorderly mess. I liked the spontaneity in that approach.

    Olly and I looked at each other in dismay and dejection. 'Were they leaving us because they had had enough

of our bad behaviour and infantile tantrums? Were we going to be dispatched to some new house and undergo another round of rigorous examination to qualify for shelter?' You know, when the mind is fearful it goes cuckoo. These were rare moments when we did not live in the moment. Both of us got panic attacks. Olly began to cry, and I went under the sofa to hide my tears. Thankfully we were assuaged soon enough when Missy and Mo came and hugged us both and said I love you a million times and then broke down in tears themselves. 'We will miss you both,' they said. And it was then that we figured that they were peregrinating to a foreign land for a holiday. They would be back soon. 'Yippee!' The separation would be painful for sure, but it would not be for long. And they would miss us sorely too. 'Fair enough,' said Olly reluctantly, now emboldened and his mojo relaunched, though he promptly went and peed on Mama's suitcase as a sign of protest. I followed suit. I chose Beard's battered and bruised red-coloured Samsonite. My pee would travel the world even if I did not.

8
THE STUDS RULE THE WORLD

'Good teaching is one-fourth preparation and three-fourths theatre.'
—Gail Godwin

Between the two of us, Olly had much higher testosterone levels. Basically, he was hornier. As we grew up into super-smart studs of our locality, I could see Olly strut around the pretty chicks, especially Pink, a sweet-faced German Shepherd who lived down the lane. Pink was an imposing exhibition of canine grace. She may have been about five times his size, but Ol was a natural charmer who believed he could seduce anyone; size did not matter. Whenever Bhola took us for walks, Olly would crane his neck to see Pink when we crossed her huge mansion (the only one in the whole of Mumbai, I assume). Often, she would be looking out of the balcony and Olly would give her a long lingering look of lust before she disappeared from his fuzzy vision. It was cute, although I never told Ol that she may have been ogling Ginger, the leprosy-coloured Labrador in our gang who Pink may have found more physically compatible. And attractive too. But Ol was irrepressible in this story of unrequited love.

Once we had visitors in our house, one of whom seemed nervous at the prospect of dealing with us, the deadly duo. Mama was calmly reassuring. 'They are as innocuous as a butterfly.' 'Really?' I thought that was an exaggerated articulation of our innocence. The moment Mama went inside to arrange for some coffee, Olly pounced on the long leg of the suited-booted man who seemed like he was sweating buckets. He shrieked out loud, but Olly had no intention of biting him whatsoever. Instead, Olly was just exhibiting the carnal desires of us folks who are denied natural outlets; he started humping his leg. And Olly could do so with spectacular passion. The poor moustachioed fellow just froze as he watched his leg being smothered by puppy love, even as Mama came around and told Olly to immediately stop his lecherous ways. Olly being the recalcitrant character he was, obeyed hesitantly. Once again, I was baffled by the double standards of humans. While they could indulge in sex behind closed doors with anyone of their choice, we were forbidden from hanging out with members of the opposite sex. Why? Although I did hear an occasional chatter about some 'mating sessions' that were being arranged for us, they never really happened. In the prime of our overpowering bursting libido, Olly and I were expected to practise immaculate abstinence. This was so damn unfair. I think they misunderstood the Gandhi in us.

By this time both Missy and Mo had graduated from looking like silly young things with ponytails and braces into petite teenyboppers with blunt haircut, purple lipsticks, and three-inch high (more than my legs) stilettos. My two princesses were looking hot in their sizzling shorts and spaghetti tops. But that meant some serious collateral damage: boys. I hated them, not

because they usually looked like chipmunks, but because the time that Missy and Mo would normally spend with Olly and me began to dwindle. Time is a finite resource, unfortunately. Trust me, this phase is not an easy adaptation. Instead of unending cuddles at all odd hours of our choice, we had to often reconcile to fleeting warm pats on the head. And those playing sessions too shortened in length, and often I would wait with the ball in my mouth for them to continue our slugfests but they seemed happy to resign quickly so that they could go back to their mobile phones. We were growing up and so were they. I wish sometimes that we never grew up, honestly. I mean that.

I think both Big Mama and Beard realized that Olly and I, pampered as we were, could not handle this attention-deficit syndrome. Thus, they decided to compensate us by indulging in frivolous distractions that would keep us hooked: rocking us on their laps, giving us massages when we did not want them, putting on some western classical music (I liked Backstreet Boys instead) believing that we liked jazz, and making us do newspaper-fights. The latter was Olly's and my favourite sport. Olly invariably won because of his sharp fangs, and I dare say, occasionally his quicksilver temper. But what we both loved the most was those joyous car rides. Oh my god, we just went ballistic, rapturous.

While we are for sure domesticated pets and can tolerate the concrete jungle, we love Mother Nature. Although we knew we were downtown dogs and all that, the fact is that Mumbai is a hard mass of bricks, metal, machine and mortar. It is a soulless city driven mostly by the love of lucre. It gets claustrophobic, particularly in those closed elevators. We were so apprehensive inside them, Olly invariably involuntarily peed out of fear. Grass is a luxury few of us can access, as all we ever walked on was hard, tarred, uneven roads. Thus, when we would sit in the car, windows pulled down, looking outwards towards the sea, letting the breeze hit our faces, we were thrilled beyond description. The terrible fumes that came from red-coloured buses were part of the deal, but that agony had to be suffered. Both Big Mama and Beard would take us out at the slightest pretext, quietly adjusting to our shifting requirements on their laps. I think they were adorable in spoiling us rotten, and Olly and I would give them millions of licks in gratitude which they gleefully accepted. Of course, it would have helped if RDX (that's the explosive nickname they had given to their rather hot-tempered driver who probably saw us as pesky occupants) did not brake the car so suddenly, and so often. Every time he did, Ol and I would collapse in a heap, with my head usually banging against Big Mama's aristocratic nose.

Honestly, life was a joyful ride, with myriad events of varying magnitude taking place all the time. Olly and I contributed liberally to the pandemonium. Like when Mama's niece came home to show off her latest electronic gadget, a laptop with a half-eaten forbidden fruit as the brand logo. Everyone crowded around it as if it was a new-born pup. Now the problem was that my dearest Big Mama was simultaneously packing her bags to go for a conference somewhere. Naturally I was in a terribly bad mood. I expressed my displeasure by plonking right on top of her trolley. The innuendo (if you want to use a subtle term) was clear to one and all: 'DON'T GO, PLEASE.' But instead of trying to mollify my wounded sentiments, everyone just went, 'Oh, look at Lou, he is so cute.' Cute, my left paw, I was hopping furious. But then they treated my disgruntlement disrespectfully. The niece did not help matters by trying to click pictures of me and asking me to pose. I studiously ignored her. I was no pushover. But soon my moment to exact revenge on this paparazzi behaviour arrived, almost with impeccable serendipity. There was an emergency. They all rushed to the kitchen where our famous cook had apparently forgotten to switch off the oven resulting in smoked banana muffins whose aroma probably wafted all the way up to the monkeys on Malabar Hill. This was an opportunity I was not going to let go. I grinned to myself, encircled the laptop once, twice, thrice, and then lifted my leg and dropped a sizeable portion of my pee on to the computer's keyboard. Then I quietly trooped to the kitchen with a sorry expression to sympathize with the cook who was being made to feel that she had just

committed a bank heist. To be frank, the burnt banana had a sexy smell. The house help (I don't remember her name as their turnover was higher than Apple Inc.) deserved a Michelin star for this nouvelle cuisine breakthrough. Anyway, I waited for the moment of epiphany when Mama's niece would discover that her keyboard had sweated under Mumbai's scorching heat. Predictably, it came within minutes.

'I think someone has dropped water on my laptop,' the young lady rued mournfully. Perhaps she had a bad case of sinus because I am very proud of my unique smell or stamp of authority. Mama looked aghast, but then she did not have a bad cold, and her first suspicions had hit the jackpot. From one end of the house, I heard her scream: 'LOOOUIIIIIIIS!' I refused to budge preferring to remain ensconced in the comfort of the sofa's underbelly. But Mama can be as adamant as me. She stood like a towering inferno in front of the sofa and ordered me to come out. 'Louis, come out, instantly. You have been a really bad boy.' Now let me tell you a secret. Ol and I had through conscientious research analysed that whenever we did something wicked and the reprimand was that either of us had been 'a bad boy', it meant that we could manoeuvre out of our predicament, our situation, if we handled it with diplomatic finesse.

Bad boy basically meant, bad for sure, but also somewhat slapstick. There was some hope. Therefore pretending to be woken up from a deep sleep, I stepped out to confront Mama, my heart palpitating away. Mama lifted me off the ground, holding me by my two front shoulders and looked straight into my eyes and muttered under her breath (mostly for her niece's benefit, I think): 'Louis, why did you do that?' From the corner of my eye, I could see Missy and Mo in paroxysm of giggles, while Beard appeared unconvinced that I, a model of decency, deserved a hollering for one minor peccadillo.

'Do what?' I wanted to ask her, but better wisdom prevailed. I looked back straight into her eyes, a personification of hurt and distress combined. I was a master of this ingenious trick. It had the desired repercussions; she looked down sheepishly, pretending to be apologetic about wrongly suspecting me of the crime (it could also be Olly, right?), while I carefully controlled my laughter. That was typical Mama, blow hot blow cold. Of course, I also knew I was the apple of her eye. After all, it was me and not Beard that she cuddled with under the blanket when we went to sleep, right? The niece felt gratified at my chastisement (although in all fairness she took the keyboard attack in her stride). The moment she left, Mama gave me a short fat chewy stick good for my gums, which had a delicious dry pork as a head. I resolved to pee more often on keyboards if I got the opportunity. I got my chance, however, to wet a sophisticated tripod instead.

Now Beard, strangely, was a politician of sorts; I say 'of sorts' because he wore well-tailored Brooks Brothers suits in the daytime and woefully ill-fitting Nehru (if someone is offended that I haven't called it something else more contemporary, go take a flying fish) jackets in the evening. Big Mama would often joke that if Beard could be a politician, then pigs could fly. While all through the day Beard would use cuss words and behave like his ancestral monkeys, in the nights he would abruptly assume an air of gentlemanliness. Basically, he would be politically correct and extremely boring after sunset. Olly and I did not like this schizophrenic behaviour of his. Worse, our house had several television crews in the evening who for some absurd reason or the other wanted to hear Beard's views on the state of the country (no one knew that nobody listened to him at home to begin with). The idiot box and Beard were an inseparable partnership. I was jealous of this and promised Olly that I would jeopardize this growing affinity. Olly was madder still because the entire drawing room would be cordoned off during this curfew time. While Beard was normally the coolest dude at most times, he would transmogrify into a sullen dour-faced yawn when the camera lights were on. I did not like this.

One evening, I quietly sneaked out when the tactless house staff left the door slightly ajar. I headed straight for the camera crew who looked flabbergasted to see me, an oversized kebab in a choleric mood. They ran helter-skelter, tripping over wires with one almost falling on Beard's lap. As it happened, the live transmission was on, so all Beard could do was give me a sharp dirty look, warning me of dire consequences later if I did not behave myself (which meant a soft whack on my buttock that was more ticklish than anything else). I ignored him and gave the tripod my signature piss. Then even as the hapless crew watched with astonishment I jumped on to Beard's lap (his bony legs were so uncomfortable unlike Big Mama's, frankly). But the principal cameraman responded with remarkable alacrity, egged on by Beard's nod, and promptly changed the camera angle. Damn! My chance to express my views on animal rights, besides inflation, rural distress, social polarization and crony capitalism on NDTV was gone.

9

MIDDLE-AGED AND ALL

'Age is a function of mind over matter.
If you don't mind, it doesn't matter.'
—Mark Twain

Now I am assuming that you already know but we are more mature corresponding compared to our human counterparts, chronologically speaking. While a three-year toddler is yet being toilet trained, we are busy and bustling teenagers, looking for a romantic infatuation. Therefore although Missy and Mo were still treating us like candyfloss and picking us up and throwing us around as if we were a volleyball needing some practice, we had actually become middle-aged. At six years, the canine on average is approximately 40 years old in the human calendar. Unknown to our illustrious Family, Olly and I were battling a mid-life crisis. That meant that we were more irritable, our bowel movements were considerably erratic, Angelina from the new neighbours in the opposite apartment was ignoring our muscular appeal, and we were mildly better behaved than in our smart-alecky years. I don't think Beard would necessarily agree with our latter assertion.

Beard loved tennis. He returned one day from the club and casually dumped his tennis bag on the sofa and went inside for a shower. I saw a chance and promptly grabbed it. Jumping on the sofa, I navigated the tight zipper with my nose (I am fairly ambidextrous) by taking advantage of a slight opening. I saw three bright yellow tennis balls in a can branded as Wilson. I had secretly cherished those balls since Beard started bouncing them against the wall, challenging me to grab them in between. But Beard was a cheapskate and only used old balls to play with me, those that he no longer needed to hit his forehand topspin. I thought that at least occasionally I could have done with more than discarded 'seconds'. A new ball is a new ball after all. Go ask Roger Federer when he is getting ready to serve. I pushed the can on to the floor and immediately the plastic black cover rolled off and three luminous fuzzy-haired yellow balls scattered in different directions. Olly and I were in a dilemma as to which one to pick and which one to leave out, so we both grabbed one each and left the other for a rainy day. I loved sinking my teeth into that fine rubbery texture, especially the part that had my initials L written on it. Soon Mo arrived and she seemed quite impressed by our chutzpah. She pulled in the third ball too and we had a real blast. New balls have a slightly better bounce and spin and it suits athletic characters with an aptitude for snatch; see, there is a complex pyrotechnic behind why I wanted them. However, our celebration was too good to last for long. I could hear Mama give Beard a dressing down for contravening clause 5 C (b.3) in her Operating Manual for good housekeeping protocol. Why had he left the tennis bag in the drawing room when there was a storage space already allotted for it? Poor Beard, I genuinely felt sorry for him. Sporting a hangdog expression, Beard soon returned to pick up his coveted possession. But on seeing the three of us play fetch with his recent purchase, he literally froze.

'Now how did this happen? I have just used them once.' When Beard got furious, he never

screamed. He just spoke with a peculiar twang that sounded like a cross between a Chinese and an Italian accent.

There was a long pregnant pause that felt like eternity. Olly and I just pretended that we had heard nothing. Mo kept smiling.

'It's not funny,' said Beard, trying hard to sound sinister. 'Who did this? Who opened my bag?' Now his accent had turned into a Mexican and Mandarin mix.

Expectedly the cynical scoundrel looked at me first. I looked back at him, unblinking, responding with a Gandhian resolve to not buckle under pressure. I borrowed his famous words from farcical TV debates he was part of. 'Stop making accusations, bro. Let the law take its own course after a transparent investigation.' Olly, unfortunately, had a perpetually guilty-looking expression on his face which was exacerbated by his ever-moving eyeballs that seemed to be on roller skates. But Beard knew that more than tennis balls, O's real squeeze was leather shoes. The needle of suspicion now fell on Mo. But fortunately, Mo knew that Beard could be rotated on the tip of her left thumb. So she valiantly rose to the occasion for us.

'Daaaad,' she drawled and I could see that the extended stretch was already having a dramatic effect on her dear papa.

'I thought the balls were old, after all you had already played with them. Anyway, if you are so unhappy, I will buy you a new tin, okay? I am the one who gave it to them. But please for god's sake, don't shout at these angels,' Mo implored her father who was now on the verge of an emotional guilt trip. And as good Samaritans, Olly and I sat there with pained expressions, which also had a forgiving disposition: 'Okay Beard, we will ignore your temporary fit of madness. Shit happens, we know.'

Beard underwent an extraordinary alteration. He promptly went to the kitchen and from the sound of plastic bags being ripped apart, we knew that the pork chewy was on its way. It was. Mo had saved us from certain disciplinary action as Beard was obsessed about his club-level tennis histrionics, sometimes dry-serving, volleying and smashing in thin air at home. When Beard came to cajole us into eating that meaty morsel, Ol and I took it from him as if we were doing him a big favour. That evening we cuddled with Mo in her room, Olly near her stomach, and me walking all over her, telling her that she was the world's best sister. But even Mo would get exasperated with me when I chased those pigeons who came visiting us every morning.

The morning routine at home was like a call centre's script—flawless to the core, scripted to perfection. The best part is it happened on account of consummate human habits. Big Mama would visit the small secular prayer room which had many gods looking calm and serious; even we refused to bark and misbehave in that consecrated space. We would follow her religiously like ardent devotees. Then she would sit in the large drawing room facing an open balcony surrounded by flowerpots, which were attractive propositions for us to clandestinely pee on when no one was looking. Beard would follow suit as if on trance, singing 'Louis Olly Re'. He was not Justin Bieber. He was not Sonu Nigam either for that matter. Then he would try and displace me from the sofa which Big Mama had monopolized using the first-come-first-served policy. His nefarious stratagems included making a fake airplane with his hand that was zooming at me like a Rafale jet that had been properly accounted for. It was accompanied by his awful pretence of being a roaring aircraft engine from the times of Pearl Harbor. Beard knew that he was deliberately instigating me but he seemed to love his morning misdemeanour. Sadist! I truly detested fireworks so early in the day. Morning was a time for meditation and spirituality, not hassling a poor lil Dachshund who was looking to protect his turf on a sofa that could at best accommodate two. Invariably, it was Mama who came to the rescue. She would help me squeeze between the sofa's back rest and her expansive thighs (thank god she wasn't into some weight loss programme), in the process throwing a mountain of newspapers towards Beard who would gleefully catch them as if he was Virat Kohli, looking very pleased with himself. Beard, who epitomized brazen shamelessness, would then

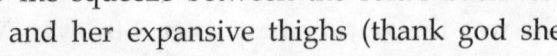

continue to tease and torment me despite Mama's warnings. Then when I would growl at him, she would say: 'Don't you get it? He doesn't think you are being funny. He hates you.' His raging enthusiasm suddenly flattened, Beard would look crestfallen at me. This was the time that I played the great do-gooder. I pretended to empathize with his sad state of affairs and botched fireworks and I would move from Mama's lap to his. At once, the sunshine smile would return and he would tell Mama: 'See how much he loves me?' Mama would ignore that. This was our daily standard operating procedure. There were two pigeons who added to this drama.

Basically, despite being a city that resembles Gotham in Batman films, Mumbai still has a few birds that have foolishly migrated here, perhaps in the hope of living high on 28-floor skyscrapers on Peddar Road and

receiving five-star treatment. Or use a helipad if they were exhausted of flying. It was an error of judgement on their part. Basically, that explains why stupid people are called bird-brained. Mumbai has atrocious buildings, each one competing with the other in grotesqueness. In short, it is a race to hell. Where do you build a nest here, parrot? Thus, it was hardly surprising that these silly birds would flock to our house because we still had patches of green, flowerpots, a mini-garden in front, and some neighbours who believed in climate change. This noisy pigeon couple, who seemed madly in love, had made our home their own too, without signing a lease agreement. They would arrive every morning and canoodle away on the top of our balcony doors. Olly and I would both chase them and bark at them, but they were smart enough to decipher our limited bandwidth. They would continue to indulge in romantic manifestations completely oblivious of our incessant barking. One day, calamity struck the lovebirds. But first, a backdrop.

Now for all his ferocious aggressiveness, Olly was the kindest soul on earth. He was an archetypal Lhasa Apso; the only thing he perhaps needed to master was pranayam. He was like a monk who sold his Maybach. But I, being from the distinguished Dachshund family of spotless German descent, was a natural-born hunter. Despite my tiny size I had a sliver of Arnold Schwarzenegger and

Sylvester Stallone in me. One fine day, perhaps carried away in their passionate ardour, one of the two pigeons fell from the door. I possessed a sharp instinct for these occasions; I leapt from Beard's lap and headed straight for my prey. As did Olly. Beard screamed: 'NO!' But who was listening? The pigeon fluttered and flapped its wings, but it had hurt itself, as it got trapped between the cleavage of the sliding glass doors. As I neared to catch my object of affection, Olly stood in the way, like an embankment. 'Olly, you okay?' I said, but he was as obdurate as the Great Wall of China. Olly just refused to let me go and do a gentle examination of the injured feast that awaited me. In fact, he got into a scrap with me, and after aeons we fought like they do on prime-time television channels, all bark and no bite. Beard, who is ill-equipped to handle matters of life and death, had summoned the building's security guard in the meantime to get into rescue operations. Afterwards, the pigeon was transported to a nearby bird shelter for rehabilitation. But the story did not end there.

When Missy and Mo woke up (which was usually just past lunch time on weekends) they heard the entire narrative of a melodramatic morning from Mama, who usually punctuated it with her own hallucinations of the event. Result: I was made to look like a vicious troll (humans of this variety are often seen as unverified eggheads on Twitter) with nefarious designs of the unholy kind. Both Missy and Mo looked at me with profound dismay, and almost concomitantly said: 'Bad boy!' I said nothing in defence against this glaring prejudice. I had not even hurt a single feather of that pigeon. I did not engineer its fall, did I? Anyway, the best way to win an argument is to avoid it, says Dale Carnegie. I followed that advice.

It was a cold January evening of 2014 and the weak winter sun had just gone behind one of the television towers in the far distance. Olly was running around aimlessly and when he was not, he was chewing newspapers that Beard used for a tug-of-war contest with him. Mama was working on her laptop, which sat on a pillow on her lap. Mo was watching a tennis match featuring her idol called Djoker. I was undecided on whether I should join Olly for our regular race around the house or look mournfully at Mo till she succumbed to my anguish, and played ball. Then the doorbell rang.

Missy walked in, looking terribly harried and upset.

'Mom and Dad, please come here. We need to do something.' As everyone rushed to the door in panic, I noticed something from my height of one foot above floor level. Nestled in Missy's arms was a brown and white ragamuffin who was no bigger than the TV remote control. It was shivering, shaking in fear or hunger or both. The creature's eyes were closed as if it was in a deep sleep. It resembled a harmless bundle of nothingness. We had a visitor.

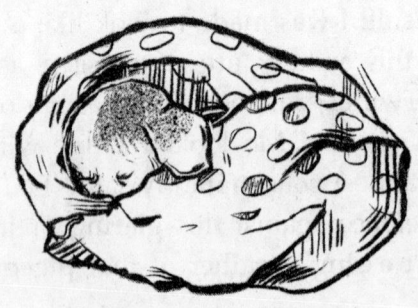

10

THE VISITOR

'If you want others to be happy, practise compassion.
If you want to be happy, practise compassion.'
—Dalai Lama

It is said that curiosity killed the cat, but as far as we were concerned it definitely strained our necks as we peeked to see who had Missy brought into the house. But more importantly, what intrigued both Olly and me was, why? We are very possessive creatures, we love to own our masters, our walk-givers, our house staff, the cooks, everybody. It is a territorial thingy; we don't enjoy sharing what we love. Ol and I were at the zenith of our happiness, fit and healthy, the Family was delightfully crazy and they adored us, and we were getting all the attention we wanted at the whiff of a sneeze. That raised "the legitimate question" (copyrighted to celebrity TV anchors): 'Who was this little brown and white rag, and why was the Family huddled around it?' Noticing that I was feeling low, Olly took me to the side, and asked me, his eyes all swelled with tears, 'Do you think we are not enough for them? Have we misbehaved too much, taken them for granted?' I comforted him by leaning against him and reassuring him that it was impossible. We were the apple (Beard would have preferred mango) of their eyes, and clearly the centre of their universe. It had to be something else. It was.

Missy had spotted the small mongrel in the popular business district of Mumbai, Ballard Estate, all alone, shrivelled with fear and hunger, desolate and abandoned. A few big dogs were terrorizing it. Some monsters had teased it by tying a handkerchief to its tail. She got spooked at the thought of leaving it alone, apprehending that it would come under a vehicle when it ran away from the mob. Not knowing what to do, she had panicked and brought it home. Our house was meant to be a temporary shelter until the mongrel was adopted. She had already posted his tear-stained puppy face on Facebook (that strategy usually worked) and appealed for guardianship. I was only worried that the users of the social media platform would not treat that as fake news.

We were both relieved to know that our duopolistic control was unchallenged. Whew! Now please don't get us wrong; he was a cute fellow, and best of all, even smaller than us. It gave us an opportunity to be both schoolmasterist and condescending for a change. Talking down (literally) was fun actually, and for me that was a novel experience. Olly for some reason did not want to engage with him at all, and either walked away or gave him one astringent growl. The poor puppy would immediately scamper for cover. I felt a sympathetic propensity for him though; he was underfed, frightened and had nowhere to go. Mama appeared agitated to have him even for a day and family tension was rising higher than even the Sensex. Missy and Mo stood resolute—dumping him back on the deadly streets was not an option. Beard understood their quandary. Olly and I hung about on our own, still grappling with this unprecedented, divided attention from the Family on account of an unusual circumstance. Then before you could say Barack Obama, the little fellow was gone. He had a home. A family had decided to adopt him. Olly and I heaved a sigh of relief. The idea of sharing our beloved Family with anyone else was nothing short of blasphemous. No way, Jose!

Around this time, both Missy and Mo were having wild house parties attended by boys with ridiculous hair (sometimes painted blue and resembling a porcupine's quills), sweaty armpits, torn jeans and cheap alcohol breath. We dismissed that as probably shabby upbringing. One of them took a shine to Olly, mistaking his Tibetan origins for anodyne comportment. When Ol bit his left hand, those notions were promptly shattered. I had my fan club too but most seemed fascinated by my long torso and tiny legs, clicking pictures of me, without obviously taking my permission. Puppyrazzi, did I get the spelling right? When they were not entertaining weirdos, the girls were returning home at unearthly hours that had Mama agitated and Beard snoring. Now we dogs love our sleep too but these interruptions were fun; we got to snack on those coveted treats for being good boys.

Through a judicious combination of feigned helplessness and a charm offensive (as you already know), I had acquired prime real estate next to Mama on the bed. Olly, because of his intermittent outbursts of ire, was given a posh residence at two of the far corners of the room, which he reluctantly occupied. To ensure that Beard did not feel that I was giving him a stepmotherly treatment, I would also sneak into his soft quilt to compensate his wounded sentiments. I could sense that Beard was placated by my presence on his half of the bed. But thanks to my presence, I contributed to India's family planning targets and ensured that population boom was not happening at home.

Then one fine day the doorbell rang and I found Missy running towards it as if she was preparing for an Olympics 100-metre sprint. A young boy who looked like a Sumo wrestler handed a small package wrapped in the same light lemon-coloured bedsheet in which it had been dispatched just a few days ago. Astonishingly, the small puppy was back. It seemed that he had cried continuously since being sent away and refused to be pacified by either milk or toys. The Family stood around him stunned with disbelief.

A long pause followed as no one knew what to do. It was what is called a gridlock.

'He is meant to be here,' said Missy breaking the impenetrable silence but almost thrilled to have him back. Mo and Beard nodded quickly in agreement.

Only my Big Mama seemed peeved. 'I am sorry. You will have to find a place for him elsewhere.'

But no home was found willing to take the fellow who looked like a small-sized sourdough bread. As time passed, the struggling homeless thing even inspired our sympathy, though not completely. Olly remained incensed at the sacrilege. He felt the house was sacrosanct and belonged just to the two of us. I was comparatively more tolerant.

A few weeks later, the light beige-coloured dog with large swathes of white patches, hazy eyes and a benign expression had wriggled itself into our home. The Family named him Pablo.

11

THE GOODBYES BEGIN

'Too often we underestimate the power of a touch, a smile, a kind word, a listening ear, an honest compliment, or the smallest act of caring, all of which have the potential to turn a life around.'
—Leo Buscagila

Pablo was as crazy and abstruse as puppies come; they drive one towards transcendental meditation. For Olly and me he was a juvenile distraction, a plaything that the Family had brought in to entertain us. Maybe Beard had silly notions of saving his delicious tennis balls and this was a bouncy alternative. And in all fairness, Pablo was a perfect flippant and frivolous plaything who obediently followed us around, till an impatient Olly would remind him of who was the boss. Our early foreboding of divided attention never materialized as the Family, all of them, never let us feel that the latest arrival would get any special privileges and even a transient elevated priority. We liked that. Immensely. Missy was particularly sensitive to our fragile temperament, fully aware that we needed the overarching shield of her addictive indulgence. After Pablo came, our cuddle-time with her increased exponentially. Both Olly and I felt blessed to be in this magical kingdom of limitless love. Time just happily rolled by, amidst summer holidays, long walks with Bhola, ballgames, our birthday parties, weekend binging on those yummy treats, wild parties at home hosted by Missy and Mo who had become such pretty damsels, expressway drives to Pune during extended weekends, and warm curling up on wintry nights. Life, as the cliché goes, was a breeze.

More than a year just rolled by desultorily and the

little kid Pablo metamorphosed into a towering figure, a bruising powerhouse of muscle. How and when he became like a basketball player, we had no idea (at least from our line of vision). Olly and I had of course remained of the same proportion, give or take a few inches of belly fat. Pablo's strapping vertical growth was similar to the tall skyscraper that had come up outside our house from nowhere, obscuring the panoramic view of the blue skies that extended towards the Malabar Hill skyline. We were initially a bit worried by the disproportionate disequilibrium it created for us as Pablo gave us immense deference. He followed us around as if we were Pied Piper, and always gave us the respect we deserved. We liked it. We loved it. We were a bigger family now, madder, more irrational, more in need of deep breathing exercises. But it was a wild ride that no one was complaining about, especially Beard who seemed to thrive in lawlessness, which corporate jargon defines as the VUCA world. Or whatever.

For Olly and me, the most difficult hours were between 10 a.m. and 6 p.m., when practically everyone was out somewhere. The girls were in college or working, and both Beard and Mama were in office. I missed them sorely although I was always proficient at impersonating as 'the' macho man. When they returned and the doorbell rang (each had a distinctive

recognizable pattern of ringing it, with Big Mama's being an extended jingle like Kanye West rapping), we went berserk. The hiatus away from them was an unbearable pain. The Family was our world, our world was the Family. We would bark and run around them right until they dropped everything and compensated us with unending affections, including rolling on the floor if we so demanded. Beard was always game for such practical calisthenics. Olly could be unmanageable; he sometimes peed in excitement although frankly, sometimes so did I. We canine species know how to express love; we are not measured or strategic when it comes to uttering sweet nothings. Love must be unmistakable, unconditional, with no expectations of a quid pro quo. Or else it is like a choreographed premediated script, where all we do is rehearse and read out our plastic lines. We are different, we think with our hearts. Nothing else matters. If only humans could understand that between the head and the heart, it is the latter that speaks to our conscience. The former is only a cold spreadsheet giving a rational SWOT analysis of a given situation. Dump it, because the variables keep changing anyway. But since I am not a Harvard Business School grad, I chose to be unassuming and kept my profound wisdom to myself. We can also make out the difference between a rushed fictitious assuagement and a genuine warm pat, even if it's momentary. Love is instinctive, one can feel it. We could. Always.

  Each one of us had a sweet spot in the house, literally, places that had our signature dominance. Olly loved the prayer room, Mo's bed and her study table, the cosy spot below the largest sofa in the drawing room and the secluded space near the piano that only he could have managed to squeeze into. Pablo was mostly ensconced in the room of his saviour Missy, who was now his unofficial Mama, but when he did venture out, he was all over the place, quite happily adjusted to playing third fiddle to his two formidable seniors. My suzerainty extended to the whole house, of course, but the kitchen, all balconies, the middle of the drawing room and the master bedroom was the Dachshund's dominion. We were all equally happy with this tranquil arrangement. The serenity though received a few jolts in between as we did not like casual trespassers. While O and I had an unwritten arrangement, Pablo had somewhat involuntarily upset that understanding. Out of the blue a few cracks had begun to surface in our sweet world. For the first time in our peaceful lives thus far, we became a bit edgy. Perhaps it was inevitable. Perhaps not.

One fine day Missy's friends arrived for an evening hangout at our home. They usually came in a raucous, jangly bunch, some actually carrying a guitar and a pair of unmusical loud drums. Naturally the three of us ran to join in the carousal. It was then that something went horribly wrong. Something unexpected, something so unpredictably horrendous that we were not prepared for it. Pablo snapped. He viciously attacked my darling soulmate, Olly. Poor Ol, he was always such a frail, fragile fellow behind that superman posture he would adopt. He was stunned and so was I. We were speechless at the violent rage that Pablo exhibited, that was so unlike him, because till then he had been a sweet, subservient, almost subjugated character, who did not have the A of anger in him. But the way he pounced on Olly was a terrifying spectacle. Although Olly received a few bites from Pablo's dracula teeth, nothing serious happened. But in those ten seconds of incendiary indignation from Pablo, something changed. And it changed our lives forever.

Olly never recovered from the psychological blow from that singular lethal skirmish; he became perpetually fearful in Pablo's presence. We dogs have long memories even if we are not as bulky as those elephants. I hated to see my best friend avoid Pablo, who after that explosive wrath of his had suddenly discovered that he was at least five times our size, and that this was not a battle of equals. Olly symbolized the fact that it is not the size of the dog in the fight that matters but the size of the fight in the dog. But this war was skewed. Overnight, Pablo knew he had the muscle power to intimidate us if he wanted to, at will. For the first time, I saw the Family worried. They had not expected this. There was anxiety in the air. Pablo had been adopted on good faith, and because Missy had the largest heart conceivable for desperate strays facing certain mortality.

I vowed to myself that if Pablo misbehaved again with Olly, I would single-handedly teach him a lesson. We were here much before him, and this was our home. We had welcomed him and helped him assimilate joyfully; was this asperity his way of expressing his gratitude? Although truce soon returned and we often played together (Pablo also joined the dog-walkers club), ate together and hung out like nothing nasty had happened, our relationship had fundamentally changed. There were new power dynamics at play and Pablo had sensed he was in the driver's seat.

As if Olly's traumatic experience was not bad enough, we were broken-hearted when we found that Missy had begun packing her clothes into big suitcases over a period of a week. This looked portentous; it did not look good at all. It did not help Olly and me much as Pablo usually was in close proximity of her, hovering around his protective Mama. We had to now approach her tentatively, unsure of the powerful Pablo's unpredictability. The Family, let me be honest, looked guilt-ridden but helpless. Anyway, our suspicions proved correct; heartbreak was round the corner.

Missy was travelling abroad for higher education. She was going to go for several months, unlike the few weeks of summer holidays that we grudgingly withstood. For Olly and me this prospect was an excruciating torture as Missy had been an angel, spoiling us bountifully, and loving us with a tenderness only a gentle warm-hearted soul was capable of. After all she was the one who had first captivated me and made me want to check out a new home. If I had had a choice, I would have stood at the door and never let her go. I can be as obdurate as the rock of Gibraltar. But then we have our limitations;

mine was my inability to physically kidnap her. The family huddled and held each other tight, bidding the big girl goodbye, moist-eyed, letting the water buckets roll. As she gave me a kiss and hug and disappeared out of vision, I reminisced the first time I had seen her, many years ago, a bubbling bundle of unruly elation who could not take her eyes off a mini-Dachshund with a twisted tail.

That night Olly and I roamed her empty bedroom where the smell of her perfume still pervaded the air. The lights were off, the windows open, and her bed, once a monumental mess, was spotlessly clean, its creases manicured to perfection, the pillows placed appropriately at the bed's centre. We missed the scrambled eggs her bed used to be. But now she was gone. We had no idea when she would return. I could see Olly swell up, and Olly being Olly, he was one big melting bag of emotions. 'She will be back soon,' I said to comfort him, as I valiantly struggled to douse my own chokes.

12

SOULMATES...FOREVER

'Death is a very dull, dreary affair. And my advice to you is to have nothing whatsoever to do with it.'
—W. Somerset Maugham

I confess I am not a morning person. Which sane individual wakes up at a godforsaken hour to go for a walk? Why should one interrupt a snooze, a slumber or a snore, freshen up, wear sneakers, have a milkshake and go out for a stroll when crows are shitting all over the place and car drivers are at their worst? Moreover, we dogs are aware of our fitness regimen. There is never a dull moment in our lives. If things become humdrum, we find ways to circumvent the tediousness. Like sleep like Rip Van Winkle. But Big Mama had found a weird gadget called an alarm clock, which rang even on weekends at 7 a.m. It was such an irritating interlude in our restful schedule. Olly and I would be hustled out for a morning walk, while she would retreat to the confines of the soft quilt. Talk of brazen discriminatory treatment of the underprivileged! In various forms, the archaic caste system was omnipresent. Beard, of course, would pretend that he never heard the musical instrument that played on fast forward masquerading as a wake-up call. It was a smart ruse. It usually worked for him, because he rarely opened the door for Bhola. Only Big Mama did.

Our walking group had now extended to seven; at this rate, Bhola would soon buy out the fancy neighbourhood with his hard cash. I usually led the pack of lazy fat fellows as I have already told you earlier, with Olly reluctantly playing team, while the others ambled along hearing Bhola's commands and ignoring him consistently. Pablo was a pipsqueak once we stepped outside, lily-livered and paranoid of crowds and the traffic. The expression that the Family used to describe Pablo was that he was a tiger at home and a pussycat outside. 'But why?' Perhaps Pablo had recurring nightmares of a childhood trauma of being separated from his dear mama on the ugly dark streets of a concrete jungle. Thus, he hated going for walks, the traffic noise and large cars and buses reminding him of his troubled early days. There was no other explanation for the split-personality behaviour of the rascal. I kind of empathized with his predicament. 'It must be so hard,' I thought, being lucky myself to have such a loving, carefree, protected environment in which I grew up from a one-inch leg puppy to a two-inch one macho man.

Bhola was collectively despised by all of us, and if Ginger had had his way, he would have been deprived of his masculine status. Olly, who looked like one of the Pirates of the Caribbean, commanded respect from all, largely on account of his haughty demeanour that said 'Don't mess with me'. No one did, except Pablo. And that too only at home.

Back home, while Olly and I were a happy twosome and had the Family's complete engrossment when it came to love showers, Pablo of course would occasionally remind us of his imposing presence. He was a proverbial bully at home where he assumed a new avatar that contrasted with his mousiness outside. But even at home Olly and I would gang up together to make sure that Pablo knew his boundaries. Together Olly and I were a robust coalition. The three of us had good times together, an occasional conflict notwithstanding, although with every passing year it was becoming more lopsided with Pablo morphing into a sinewy powerhouse. Somewhat concerned with the intermittent social tensions in the house, Big Mama had a brainwave to tame the tormentor; she got him castrated. We also thought that was a masterstroke. And trust me, for months later, Mr Pablo was almost like Mary's little lamb, barring an infrequent snarl that we dismissed as nothing more than some bad stomach gas. The Family essentially felt that the kerfuffles were harmless even when on a few occasions, they did get noxious. We trusted their judgement. If anyone knew what was good for us, the Family did. We loved them. And we were clearly their world too. If they thought we were safe, we were safe. It was as simple as that.

Our world was, however, disconcertingly enough,

beginning to change. Almost imperceptibly, Mo the little midget of the Family who was once affectionately called the Dosa Queen (she ate a dozen of them non-stop) had grown up big enough to start working in a bank. That meant longer hours away from home. Now this is what you call a double-whammy; after Missy went abroad to do her MBA, this was a severe blow because often in the day Mo would pack all three of us in her room. She demonstrated political management of an exceptional variety: Olly would be on the top of the bed near the pillow, with Pablo and I on opposite sides of her, with me precariously hanging by the side. It is a miracle that only one of us would suddenly cascade on to the floor on an average of twice a week. Of course, Mo would be invisible under the blanket. We were like four lethargic loafers on Noah's tottering ark. It was an ideal coalition government. We all needed each other for stability.

Now with Mo reappearing only past our dinner hour, we had more time to twiddle our thumbs. This is when the stress of loneliness began to get to me, and I think I started gorging on those Royal Canine goodies. Olly followed suit, but I think he had an enviable metabolism; he remained as athletic as one can get. I started to bloat somewhat, which meant that my tummy started teasing the floor awkwardly, although I still was the fastest on the bed and off it, and the birds knew who to keep a safe distance from. But I cannot deny that sometimes late at night in bed, I began to get a slight discomfort in my left hind leg, a peculiar pain, neither severe nor startling, but it was there. I gave the first insinuation of it to the Family by requesting for assistance sparingly when wanting to climb the sofa, to which they were more than happy to acquiesce as it gave them some m o r e excuse to crush me under their body weight, these silly ogres. But honestly, my image of being the perennial superhero without underpants, the consummate Mr Reliable being questioned, was hurting me. No one took serious notice of my physical debilitation and early signs of osteoporosis. We mini-Dachshunds are prone to spinal degradation. It is a hereditary thing, just like Beard blaming his sweet father for the scanty rainforest on his head.

Beard would walk out every morning after an evidently deep sleep, singing loudly for London to hear, 'Louis Olly P' (this was his act of political correctness and inclusive politics after Pablo had entered the family). That was a clarion call to us three heralding his majestic arrival. Mama, who was used to meditative silence in the morning, would nonchalantly dismiss the jarring disquietude created by him. Beard would try and spend time with all of us equally. I can't deny that there was a soothing warmth in his touch, although for some obtuse reason he perpetually wanted to hassle us. I would often see Olly ignore him and look philosophically outside the balcony at Mumbai's anarchic traffic, an imperturbable little Lhasa Apso perhaps reflecting life of his cousins in the quiet bucolic land of his origins, far away from the madding crowds. I was aware that Beard genuinely believed that he was a dog-whisperer. If he just knew how to whisper. Often when he spoke in his normal audible level, Big Mama would need earbuds. You can very well imagine our medical condition.

Now what I am going to tell you is a nebulous, hazy memory of mine and yet, ironically enough, one that I will never forget. It was a lazy summer afternoon, and we were all leisurely enduring the surly weather together. Missy had returned home during her annual semester break, so it seemed like good ole times, as if nothing had changed. She was the typical spoiler by birth, I think. I was in Mo's room generally doing the usual sniffing around, when I heard the doorbell ring. Almost instinctively, I rushed outside. See, we dogs are programmed for responding to any and every stimulus, especially because incurable optimists that we are, we believe that magic awaits us on the other side of the door. As I emerged onto the mouth of the hallway, Pablo too came darting in from Missy's bedroom, probably driven by the same expectation of a dazzling surprise. We collided. These sudden accidental meetings when we were both not anticipating the other in our way, had often been misunderstood by Pablo as a deliberate confrontationist attitude by me or Olly. It was as if we wanted a hostile takeover of his otherwise sacred space. That was actually never the case. Normally after a brief pause, an awkward eyeball to eyeball stare, both of us would simmer down and go our way peacefully, without anyone even noticing the inflammatory tension of a few seconds ago. But as Murphy's Law perhaps correctly postulates, if anything can go wrong, it will. It did that day.

This time Pablo seemed unusually incensed, his blood on the boil at seeing me in the middle of his path. I had never seen him look as ferocious as he did. I did not even get a moment's breath to understand why he was so truculent, when he pounced on me, pushing me to the floor on my back. I tried to extricate myself out of his heavy body weight right on top of me but it was of no avail. It was like a bulldozer on a tricycle. I could see his enraged expression, indignantly looking down at me, but I knew from experience that after a few seconds the stupid guy would just become as tractable as a marshmallow. So I just laid back, waiting for the unwarranted air turbulence to fly past. It almost did, but then I had not bargained for my best friend to come to my rescue. Olly, unable to bear seeing me pinned to the ground, leapt on Pablo. A tiny ten-and-a-half-year-old Lhasa Apso weighing all of 8 kilograms at the most, and one who could not hurt a fly, was trying to take on a guy at least five times his size. On an ordinary day, Olly was as innocuous as a butterfly on a daffodil. Remember how he saved that pigeon? But Pablo felt threatened, as if he was now in a disproportionate numerical combat, of two against one. Without wasting a second, he swiftly turned away from me and attacked Olly, who had got hold of his legs, the maximum height he could possibly reach. But thankfully the fisticuffs were all over in a few seconds. Missy and Mo restored order, and peace prevailed. Pablo walked away as if nothing had happened, and Olly and I, still rattled by the savage attack on both of us, were picked up and carried away to Missy's room for a quick health check-up. The good news: there was only a minor bruise on Ol's back and fortunately, there was no bleeding at all. And he looked hale and hearty and ready for a marathon race. The girls heaved a sigh of relief. Olly and I looked at each other, and I said: 'Thank you, brother. I love you.'

'You think I would have let that brute hurt you, Louis? Never. No one can ever hurt my best friend until I am around,' said Olly.

I felt like the luckiest dog in the whole world. I was blessed.

Soon Bhola arrived and we all went out for our afternoon walk, with Olly showing remarkable group leadership, walking ahead like how a cricket captain goes out for a toss. Olly the Superman was indeed a superstar. No one could have imagined that little Olly had fought a bull-headed ruffian just half an hour earlier. But unknown to us all, the Superman was actually in awful pain. He was haemorrhaging. He was bleeding internally, profusely, although there were no visible symptoms of the terrible damage to his organs. But true to form, the brave heart refused to share his agony. No one noticed that he had barely eaten, was strangely quiet, and was not his usual effervescent self when the doorbell rang later that evening and Beard and Big Mama returned home. In fact, he was barely to be seen, hiding himself, and hiding his unbearable anguish.

It was late at night when I jerkily woke up from a nightmare to hear a worried Family in animated conversation. Missy and Mo were inconsolable, Beard had stepped out to get the car and Big Mama looked an awful mess. Something had gone terribly wrong. My worst fears were coming true: Olly needed immediate medical supervision. He was in danger. As the Family rushed him out to the veterinary hospital, I saw my best friend looking exhausted and sleep-deprived, but he was still concealing his harrowing lesion. And even through that mayhem and madness, his agony and anxiety, he smiled at me, and said: 'I will be back, silly Lou. Now stop looking so worried, for heaven's sake. Just wait for me.' Before I could even say 'take care Ol', he was taken out of the door.

I waited for several hours at the main door, for the sound of the car, the doorbell, footsteps, an elevator climbing to the second floor, Big Mama's trademark laugh, Missy and Mo's banter, Beard's archetypal clearing of the throat, or Olly's familiar bark. I wanted to hear anything routine that I had heard a million times before. But nothing came. No one barked. I hid my tears, suppressed my fears, and pleaded to all the gods in the prayer room to let my big brother come home soon. I wanted my inspiration back, his small front and back legs outstretched, his sweet eyes darting around the room waiting for an opportunity to play mischief. His curmudgeonly demeanour that he often deliberately adopted concealed a heart of gold. Olly would let me win the newspaper-tearing wars, choosing to lose, just to make me, his overtly competitive brother, happy. He was an apotheosis of magnanimity who would even tolerate Pablo's idiosyncratic excesses. I had grown up under Ol's guidance, although I bullied him so often because he simply let me. I was still dreaming of Olly and me doing a wrestling contest on Missy's bed when the doorbell rang. It was Bhola. It was morning. Olly was not yet home. He would not return for the next six days.

The house felt eerily empty, and those few days that he was in the hospital felt like eternity. From the look on the face of the Family it was difficult to gauge what was really going on. Everyone looked downcast, but Beard exuded a luminous optimism. Was he genuinely sanguine or was it subterfuge? I felt lost and lonely even when everyone was trying so hard to cheer me up. I got meat balls, fried eggs, extra chicken with bread and was carried around everywhere. Pablo sulked in the corner, totally oblivious of the consequences of his stupidity, his irrational tantrum and flare-up that had happened without any provocation. In all fairness to the Family, albeit they chided him, they did not make him feel like a monster either. I missed Olly. I cried myself to sleep, my paws crossed, remembering that famous snarl that had greeted me when I had first come home.

Olly indeed kept his promise and came back home. But there was no bark. His tail was not wagging incessantly. That famous rumble was missing. The bite? Forget it. He was wrapped in his favourite pink towel in which he dried himself after a shampoo bath. But he was not bouncing around any more. His lovely white curls enfolding bubbles as he sprayed water droplets at everyone around him, were now asleep. Like him. He was dead.

I remembered the first day that I had come home, and how Ol had welcomed me, helped me through that teething period of acclimatization among the complex human species. I was flooded with his memories as I watched him, now lying inanimate, unaffected by the howl of the cars, the rustling of the trees, the little fly hovering near his tail. Our pee-wars, walks with Bhola, eating from the same bowl, those frenetic Usain Bolt sprints around the house, long drives to Pune, irritating Big Mama by doing our own number, and those weeks of crying on each other's shoulder when the Family was on vacation. I thought of the times when Ol would look out at Mumbai's noisy roads, his nose flat-pressed against the windowpane, his flocculent hair blowing in the direction of the breeze. He looked like a 1970s' countercultural hippie. Now, he lay motionless, his tiny soft paw jutting out of the pink cloth in which his gossamer shagginess was draped. I felt like telling him: 'Wake up and growl, Olly, fight with me, snarl at me, make a demand for a chicken bone, anything, please, one last time.'

I had no idea that we had been together for a decade. But wasn't it just the beginning? Don't these imperfect humans live till they are hundred? 'We had more in store,' I thought. Endless love does not deserve a grand finale act so early.

The Family made me sit next to him, perhaps to prepare me for what lay ahead. A life without my partner. My best friend. My soulmate.

My last image of Olly was Missy and Mo together carrying him in their arms as he departed for his last car ride—a drive to Pune where he would be buried alongside Amadeus in the family home. 'Goodbye my friend, we will meet again one day I know.' I wish I could do that now, Olly, but who will take care of these crying monkeys?

That night I could not sleep, as I shuddered at the thought of waking up in the morning without my best buddy's friendly hugs and cuddles, followed by the usual morning routine. Later that night, I heard soft footsteps that startled me. It sounded exactly like Olly was somewhere there. Or was I just imagining things? I have no idea but I battled these spectres for a long time after. They lasted for months. The cruel thing about death is its finality. There are no comebacks. It transcends life. Olly had gone into the beyond. An afterlife. And I had to figure out how to overcome his loss and put on a brave face. For the sake of my family, I would do anything. Life tests you, and by now you know, I hate to be on the losing side of things. With Olly still by my side from the heavens above, I knew that there was no giving up.

13

WTH IS WFH

'Be a master of your petty annoyances and conserve your energies for the big, worthwhile things. It isn't the mountain ahead that wears you out—its the grain of sand in your shoes.'
—Robert Service

O was the X factor in my life, and I felt a gnawing vacancy in my heart in the months following his death. It was indescribably difficult. I lost my appetite, did not enjoy walks any longer, and it needed a lot to cajole and convince me to fall for the several distractions the Family tried to cheer me up. Frankly, I was in a dark place. As they say, it's okay to not be okay. Mo, who seemed particularly worried about me after Olly's tragic loss, was not going to take any chances. She took me, much against my wishes, for a medical check-up. It shockingly revealed that I had kidney stones, and early traces of cancer. I needed immediate surgery, as the risks were mounting. Within two weeks of Olly's death, I was in the same hospital too. It seemed unreal. Frightening. The Family looked distressed. Their world had drastically altered, although they fought back tears when they were with me. But I am a scrappy fighter. I went through a minor incision, after being given some narcotics, I think. 'Wasn't that Pablo's territory?' In one week, I was back home. Ready to take on life. I had to do it for Olly. And my Family.

The magic formula (or what's your poison, as humans say) to get me to get going again was rather uncomplicated: playing catch and fetch with Beard's tennis balls. That was my single-biggest addiction, my cocaine moment, so to say. The Family created a whole rack of used tennis balls, where in all fairness, Beard of his own volition contributed liberally after  returning from the club. They were all trying to spoil me wholesale, as the expression goes. It was so easy to decipher whether Beard had had a good day at the courts or if he had been pummelled to bits by a more talented, mostly younger opponent. When he won, Beard would walk in humming some Bollywood song to himself but loud enough for the world to hear (usually from a Shah Rukh Khan film); when he lost, he would walk in and dump his bag straight into the cupboard, and then sit and sulk on the sofa, muttering to himself (using some Punjabi expletives) and playing tennis shots in thin air, reminding himself to not goof up his backhand slice the next time around. And mundane stuff like that. It was when Beard won that he would donate balls generously into my treasury. No one else in the house monitored his mood swings more than me, because somehow, I felt that if I had regrettably been born as a human, I probably would have been like him: cocky, self-assured but overwhelmingly condescending, extremely competitive, disdainfully dismissive of stupid behaviour, and perpetually bouncing off the walls for no apparent reason. He was my alter ego. Of course, I was much better-looking than him, my handsomeness remaining unmatched. Beard looked like a sophisticated version of a

Bollywood goonda from a C-grade crime caper produced in Jhumritalaiyya (please google the state of Jharkhand for further details of this place). How he landed up with the more stylish, sophisticated and upscale Big Mama was a conundrum. 'Seriously!' I mean that.

Despite Olly not being there, Beard continued his early morning croon of 'Louis Olly P'. I liked that, it was reassuring that somewhere Olly was still alive in an invisible form, watching over me, taking care of his little stubborn brother. Pablo and I had established a diplomatic equation by now; in political parlance it is called 'cold peace'. We played when he had to, but the moment I felt that he was stiffening up and behaving moronic because I had cleverly outwitted him, I would leave him to live with his demons. A few seconds later, Pablo would wag his tail earnestly and with a forlorn face that looked terribly embarrassed would come and say, 'Why did you stop playing with me?' He would be truly apologetic.

He meant it, I know. I would consent to resuming games with the overgrown callow fellow after playing hard to get for a while. But as time passed, Pablo had started to mellow down, frequently demonstrating that he was getting over his erratic tempestuous temper. All was well.

One regular evening I saw the Family huddled up around the television set where a septuagenarian silver-haired man with a flowing beard seemed to be pontificating on something rather grave. They looked anxious. It was followed by a deathly silence. A few days later the roads were thoroughly deserted, traffic vanished completely, and those ear-splitting sounds vaporized into thin air. A peculiar psychosis seemed to have gripped the usually grating and intolerably noisy human species. Something was certainly amiss; how come they were suddenly becoming so temperate? Whatever it was, it had a collateral consequence of gargantuan magnitude where Pablo and I were concerned; the Family stayed at home 24x7. It was just incredible. They just did not step out of the house at all. Now this was the kind of heavenly intervention I had secretly prayed for all my life. And God had responded favourably to my wishes at last. Yes, it is true that they did drive us up the wall often, in fact, right up to the ceiling fan, usually overdoing their 'concern act'. Especially when I ate less than normal, or my pee was mustard-coloured or when I would throw up at night because of the pigeon-feather that I had secretly gulped down. But we love our family always. We knew nothing beyond them, barring visiting relatives, occasional friends and regular support for household chores.

I was thrilled that they were now captive prisoners in their own home. So was Pablo. Missy had returned abroad and I missed her, but now I had Mo, Mama and Beard as my 24x7 guardian angels. And to think I had to thank some weird virus from Wuhan in China for that! Trust me, it is a mad, mad world out there. I think we dogs are the sanest. We spread love, humans transport trouble. China's export-led economic growth model included Covid-19..

The home party began in deadly earnest once the Great Lockdown was announced; late nights, late mornings, lazy afternoons, and since Bhola was now on forced leave (no one was allowed to even step out for a bit), no walks either. Also, Big Mama who was the most peripatetic of the lot, was now grounded. Mo was stationed at home, but since she was like us a sleep monster, she seemed secretly electrified with the new circumstance. Of course, it was not all honey, milk and roses as they still stared into a dumb computer screen, their laptops barking sounds from several people straitjacketed in square holes. It was called something that rhymed with doom. But it was okay. They were still at home, though. I kept hearing 'WFH' from them all the time—what the hell was that? As for Beard, for him nothing had changed. He was still doing his own number, writing copiously, looking pleased with himself for no logical reason, and doing TV shows wearing headphones that camouflaged his receding hairline. In the absence of a barber, his hairstyle reminded me of a Tamilian superstar having a bad hair day. There was one conspicuous development: during this surreal time, whenever someone came home or went

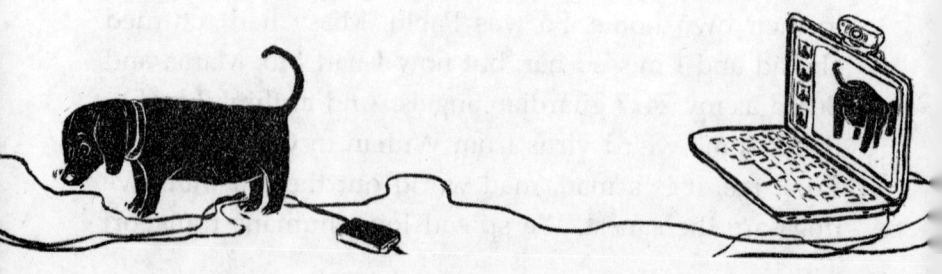

out which was rare, they wore a mask. I figured that the virus had given them a foul mouth smell. Wouldn't it be easier if they brushed their teeth with more fluoride? Look at us, we never brush our teeth, ever, and yet are invited to lick their faces.

For the first few months we had a real ball, literally and figuratively, as the Family, unaccustomed to being locked down at home, probably needed us more because we provided them with both a playful distraction and extravagant empathy. Neither Pablo nor I were complaining about their unusual quandary that we hoped would extend indefinitely. I played tennis ball games with Mo and Beard, and Pablo just slept and slept, becoming as 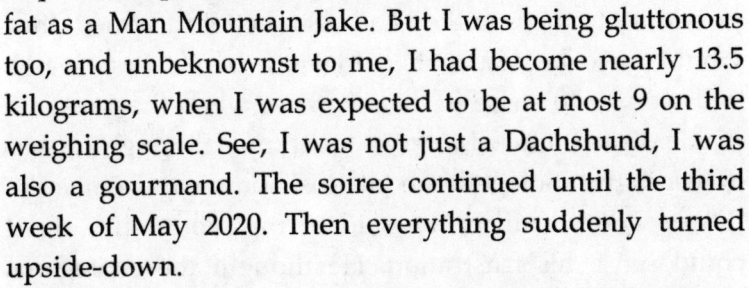 fat as a Man Mountain Jake. But I was being gluttonous too, and unbeknownst to me, I had become nearly 13.5 kilograms, when I was expected to be at most 9 on the weighing scale. See, I was not just a Dachshund, I was also a gourmand. The soiree continued until the third week of May 2020. Then everything suddenly turned upside-down.

Two men wearing ominous-looking hazmat suits of blue colour marched menacingly into our home. I was bewildered to see these hideous-looking astronauts in our home, grim-faced, and clearly harbingers of bad news.

'Why are they in our home?' I wondered. My heart sank; they headed straight for Beard. It seemed that the unseen diabolical vector called Covid-19, a form of coronavirus, had infected him. And from the worried-sick expressions on the faces of the Family, I figured that there was reason to be feel spooked out. It appeared that there was no cure for this toxic disease, and no vaccine either. We did not need another perfect storm for sure at this point in our lives. This did not look good. I suddenly started praying that maybe it was better if the Family returned to work. I could not risk Beard falling ill. He was far too clumsy for his own sake, honestly.

For the next two weeks, Beard, and for some obscure reason Mama too, went into separate rooms and remained sequestered inside. Fourteen full days, that is a staggering 336 hours of introspection, ladies and gentlemen. It was crazy, as Pablo and I would keep vigil outside their rooms waiting for an opportunity to sneak in, but even when they opened their doors, they remained not just circumspect, but defiant about our not being in close proximity to them. If they had been better informed, they would have known that a dog is a man's best friend, and we like to share in their worries when they are in a pickle. Beard refused to even touch me, although he was exceedingly apologetic about this nonsensical embargo. 'I love you so much,' he said to me repeatedly, and I could sense his frustration. He thought the contagious virus would infiltrate me too, unawares that I am very thick-skinned. Beard being locked up in a room was akin to a chimpanzee living in forced solitary confinement.

During this dull depressing phase, it was little Mo

who became the big boss of the house, marshalling resources, ordering medicines, fixing menus, ensuring cleanliness, and frequently checking on her ailing parents. She also pampered us both, pandering to our basic animal instincts, knowing fully well that we were equally distraught and disoriented. Late at night, however, she would break down into unending sobs, the perpetual anxiety of the time getting the better of her. At that time, she would pick me up and snuggle me next to her, and I would burrow my face in her curly tresses, crying along with her, but comforting her, nevertheless. Big Mama and Beard would be fine, I reassured her, although I was myself frightened as hell as to what was going on.

I will never forget the morning that they both emerged from what appeared to be an interminable hibernation. At last, it was like the return of good times. Happy times. The way we had always been. I could understand them being away during holidays when they left the city, but being at home, and being 'quarantined', as they called it, was nothing short of punishment. Anyway, we naturally know how to live in the moment (no repeated affirmations are needed), so Pablo and I had survived the ordeal. We were just elated that the nightmare was at last over. Mama and Beard were out of danger and would soon be as fit as a fiddle. Unfortunately, now I was not.

As I told you earlier, I had been hogging away shamelessly during the lockdown phase. With Bhola missing and there being strict restrictions on even casual walks around the building, even the Family's laboured endeavours to entertain us while on a leash were curtailed (they could have tried harder though, in retrospect). But when Beard and Big Mama went into their rooms for their self-isolation, life came to a near standstill for us, literally. Our movements froze. We just slept, ate, walked around the house, slept, stood outside their rooms praying for them, and ate, and slept. Mo played with us whenever she could between her maddening work schedule, but we were both turning into lazy laggards. The slug was sluggish and not complaining. It was the new normal. Occasionally, I could now feel with rising frequency a shooting pain, particularly in my left leg, when I took those long lunges from the sofas. And climbing them using my regular long-jump strides was becoming increasingly torturous. I hated to ask for help. But now I needed it. Love me, love my dog, I was telling the Family. They did. But this was not right. Something was giving way.

One breezy monsoon evening when the acclaimed Mumbai rains had eased somewhat, Mo took me for a post-dinner walk. Normally, I waited with breathless anticipation for walks whenever the Family accompanied me. They let me do my own thing. I could pee and poo at leisure unlike with Bhola and his impatient tugs. But on this day, I felt exhausted, a leg cramp developing into a soreness even on my right leg. The spirit was willing, but the flesh was weak would be a more germane description of the way I felt. But I pushed along. I was a hard-core alpha male, remember? In hiding my emotions and concealing my vulnerability I could beat Tom Hanks (though not Olly) in *Forrest Gump*. But when I returned home, the pain became insufferably bad. My left leg felt very weak, as if I was losing my ability to hold it together. I was beginning to lose my balance. I just sat there on the floor in my favourite place where I usually rested after a long walk. For a while no one seemed to notice as everything was happening as per pro-forma. Then Mama called out to me to follow her in the room for sleep-time, which I would quietly acquiesce to on a regular day. I tried to do just that, but I realized I could not. I could not push my left leg at all; it felt limp, lifeless. I could not even hobble. I was paralysed.

    I saw everyone's faces surround me; their worry made me feel even worse. But there was nothing I could do. Mama picked me up and carried me to bed. Beard and Mo were heartbroken, going by their mien. I barely slept that night wondering what the morning would bring in its wake.

    I was rushed to a veterinary hospital in the morning by Mo and Beard, who drove the car as if he was Lewis Hamilton who did not know where the brakes were. I felt so sorry to see their two sad faces trying gallantly to look brave. But being loved by them was always a huge high even if I was unable to kick ass. 'Every dog has his day,' I said to myself, 'my time will come too.' I convinced myself that a turnaround begins with an indomitable willpower. I was not going to surrender to some muscle atrophy. Ever. Giving up is a permanent solution to a temporary problem is what I had heard. I was resolved to find my way out. 'We love you, Lou-poo,' they sang a tuneless Grammy nomination number as the car drove into the hospital compound.

The tyros dressed in depressing blue overalls in the compact-sized hospital took me inside. The most challenging part was being separated from your dearest Family when you needed their presence and reassurances the most. They stretched me on a cold hard table. The doctor examining me looked like a school dropout, although he exhibited the pretensions of being a seasoned hand. To be frank, I missed old man Rustam, his high-ceilinged colonial-style clinic, with giant clocks and a soporific environment that was so feel-good. Rustam may have been straight-faced and easily riled by my bad behaviour but whenever I went there for my regular check-ups, I felt I was in the tender caring hands of a veteran. It contrasted with the steely demeanour of a man who perhaps did not want to get too emotionally involved with the eccentricities of the canine in front of him. Perhaps he had seen many come and go. But in these modern chic hospitals where they had the latest gilded gadgets, sleek machines that looked like a television set having a bad stomach upset, an operation theatre and glitzy posters promoting dog food made by multinational companies, what seemed to be missing was emotional intelligence itself. These guys were merchants of transactions, following a process where establishing

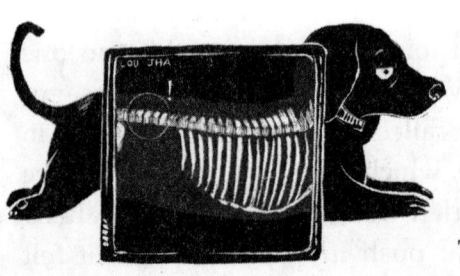

warmth with your four-legged one was not in the playbook. Sure, they were looking after me and doing the best they could, but their best was not good enough. I missed Rustam, but eventually the Family knew what I needed most. And I trusted them with my life.

My blood-work revealed that I had an irreversible kidney problem (maybe I was having too much of those omelettes from Beard's generous helpings and not drinking that boring water enough). It was further suspected that I was symptomatic of this corny alphabet soup called IVDD. That complex acronym stood for canine intervertebral disc; my long back had a problem, in short. All the running, jumping on and off of highrise sofas and the bed and landing on a slippery marble floor for over a decade was responsible for this ominous diagnosis. The gloom was lifted substantially though when the doctor said, 'If you give him regular physiotherapy and change his dietary plan (aaghhh!) he should be able to walk again. He is a fighter, let me tell you.' I don't think he noticed but at that moment I gave him a look that said 'Thank you, Mister'. Goals motivate me. And I hate losing. 'Game on,' I told myself. Self-belief is the foundation of our capabilities. Hope is the beginning of triumph.

The toughest part was that I was now deprived of that rubbery chicken gravy with liver chunks and my favourite obsession, egg yolks. Proteins were a go-slow, so all I could have was some diluted milk. I was on a renal diet, if you please, which was like eating shit on toast. Since I obdurately refused to entertain that stench, Beard started conning me by putting some chicken curry in it, which overwhelmed that unpalatable rubbish quite a bit. We struck a compromise deal and it was beginning to work. The whole house and the Family made me their priority. I was going to be fine. Missy called from abroad several times and we chatted on the WhatsApp video call for free (and no one could snoop into our conversation, either).

I started visiting a physiotherapist in suburban Mumbai (I was a townie, remember?). The drive to her place was itself like travelling to the moon and back. But then I loved drives, so I could suffer the traffic jams, endless honking and those sudden jerks ahead of speed bumps that the good driver nonchalantly drove over. And I was going through this back-breaking drive to fix my back! That's Mumbai for you. The physio followed a standard routine; she would sweet-talk me with an affected profligacy of affection. I would get an acupuncture, some laser treatment, be told to walk (which was an unnecessary addendum) and on a few occasions, swim. At home, I had to follow a regimented exercise that tested me considerably. The Family shared responsibility for the same although I concede Beard was fanatically obsessed about it. He kept everyone on their toes. The crazy Family also came up with a ridiculous-looking walking cart, apparently my wheelchair. A few months of a disciplined push and I was beginning to show signs of improvement. My pain had dissipated and my balance was now significantly better. I was getting there. Mend it like Alpha.

As the pandemic's onslaught began to diminish, the mood became merrier, chirpy. I felt it too. I still struggled and had to push myself, but I was bouncing back. Slowly and steadily, as cricket commentators would often say. Truly, my adorable Family had helped a lame dog over a stile. Literally. The Family then announced that we would be going to Pune for a month, that salubrious city with verdant lawns, blue skies and wonderful insects, besides a competitive cat around the house. Plus, Olly was there too. We had a lovely large bungalow there, and Pablo and I were both excited for making that trip after seven months of being cooped up in the cramped Mumbai bubble. I was excited about the 160 km drive ahead. I  could not wait to see the open fields, endless stretch of an expressway and the hilly breeze brush wildly against my partially open eyes. I was on cloud nine. Life was looking up. At last.

14

PURE MAGIC AND THEN...

'There are two ways to live: you can live as if nothing is a miracle; you can live as if everything is a miracle.'
—Albert Einstein

Pune was sublime from the moment we descended from the three-hour drive on to the pebble-stoned pathway that led to gardens on both sides of our family bungalow. The first thing we did was water the plants, which shone bright green as a result of our generosity. I, of course, struggled to hit the target zone because I would easily lose balance. I was astonished at Pablo's ability, however, to successfully control his enormous tank for so long. For me, recuperating from my immobility, our Pune house was a godsend. We had a large playground to meander in and the grass was pure intoxication; fluffy and well-manicured. I loved rolling on it, in the process getting my back scratched as well. I could sense my energy levels were getting enhanced, my appetite blossomed, and both my legs were getting stronger, which led me to assuming a more stable posture. After months of dragging, within weeks I was now able to stand without any support whatsoever, prompting everyone to look at me with both wonderment and spontaneous exultation. I was now recovering at a rapid rate that surprised me as well. Pablo had completely stopped quarrelling with me since I had become unwell; for one, I was no longer an impediment to his wild adventurous bouts, and secondly, because he missed my companionship during playtime. I must confess that he probably felt a bit neglected because practically everyone fussed entirely over me. I didn't mind that, obviously.

I loved my recovery routine in Pune: early morning breakfast with Big Mama, afternoons hanging out with Beard who was only too happy to walk me around the house whenever I wanted to, with Mo punctuating it with her trademark squeezes wherein she blackmailed me into giving her kisses galore. Missy kept a check on my recuperation with video calls marinated with her trademark coddling. The security guard also took a liking to me, giving me some rotis with chunks of mutton when no one was around. The winter sun felt like a palliative balm on my convalescing frame; I began to feel like the Louis of old. The protein was returning, my mojo was getting ready for a grand redux.

The Family did a back and forth from paradise (Pune) to pandemonium (Mumbai, where else?) for the next few months, which fortunately was progressively favouring the pensioner's Shangri-la. Since now I was nearly seventy years in their human calendar, Pune was my default habitat for the future, and the Family seemed favourably inclined to that prospect. I guess their only dilemma was that they could not order truffle Taglierini pasta and seabass roasted in Japanese aromatics from their downtown restaurant in Mumbai. Either way, since they had become infuriatingly disciplined

MY ILLEGITIMATE SON

in not succumbing to my teary-eyed supplications, I cared a damn. It served them right. I missed eating mouthfuls of the Provencal lamb ragout, too, isn't it?

The best news after aeons added to my sunshine disposition; after over a year since I last saw her, and after what seemed like a generation gone, Missy was to come home from abroad, where she was now hoping to become an official resident in a North American country much against my wishes. After thirteen months, we were finally all together again. My spirits soared, my enthusiasm quadrupled, my happiness was boundless, and so naturally my legs began to walk. Hurray! I was back with a bang (pardon the hackneyed expression). The only downer was that Missy's holiday was over in a jiffy, and she was leaving even before I could say 'Jack Robinson', whoever this guy is. I did not like Missy going away, not at all. I had seen her after ages. And I had no idea when I would see her again. When she said bye to me for the last time, she had no idea how I smothered my sadness. In her face, I saw the same reciprocal sentiment. We were after all inextricably interlaced by destiny. Inseparable. For the record, I hate saying goodbyes.

Then around April Fool's Day in 2021, it appeared that the virulent virus was swallowing the humans up in big gulps all over again. There was panic everywhere, and it was recommended that everyone wear a double-mask; now their mouth odour was definitely disagreeable. 'Isn't mouthwash easier?' But then humans have always been capricious. They neuter us to contain our erotic fury when we are in our best reproductive phase, but instead of getting themselves castrated, they go seek some expensive guru who gives them sermons on anger management. Level playing field, anyone? Whatever the case might be, we soon packed our bags and were on the road to Pune again, a journey I cherished and looked forward to. Mumbai was claustrophobic, Pune was commodious. Beard was driving, Mo was in the front seat, and I was sandwiched in between Mama and the laptop. Pablo was having first class seats in another car; before a journey started, he would go berserk with excitement. He was like a bull in a china shop, extremely hard to control. Mama insisted on playing western classical music on the car's stereo system because she knew I liked it too. Soon we were both enjoying our afternoon siesta. Mo reverted to her headphone to listen to some country music while Beard, thankfully, focused on the empty expressway ahead, quite happy to be delineated from music politics. He was humming with the music playing on the stereo.

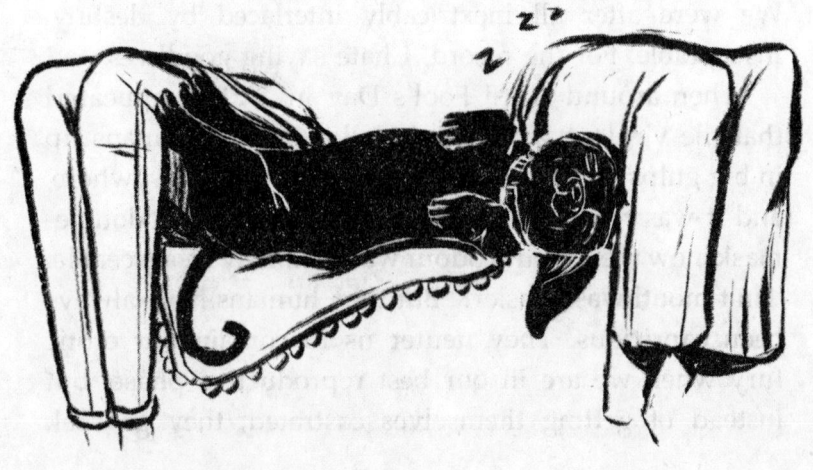

The first thing I did on reaching Pune was step down gingerly like Neil Armstrong on the moon. Then I decided to walk around the entire house on my own. I did. I needed no support whatsoever, no sling, nothing, only an occasional motivational call from Beard who would always be following me like my shadow. 'Stalker!' And Pablo would accompany me too, equally thrilled that we were back to our old times. Which meant we would pee on each other's tributaries in turns till our bladders went dry. On noticing my rediscovered pyrotechnics, our caretaker beamed with joy. 'Chamatkar,' he said. It was. I, Louis Jha, was back. I was walking. I was even running. And I was back to leaping off the sofas if I even glimpsed a furry yellow ball that got Djokovic and Federer into a marathon hitting fest on ESPN.

While humans take years on the treadmill, eat disgusting disagreeable grub for months for a measly weight loss, I was now down to my prescribed weight of 9 kilograms, looking very much like James Bond; ageing but irresistible. Sexy, basically. Life was one big get-together at home; but we remained circumspect as the sounds of ambulances began at dawn and refused to stop even after midnight hours, when the world slept. It was disconcerting this thing that they called the 'second wave'. It was hard for humans. Unknown to my Family,

I prayed for their life and health every day before I finally crashed out, leaning against my Big Mama's body, with Beard frantically playing chess online and getting checkmated, which was obvious from the terrible cuss words he used. 'What a loser, Beard!' Funnily, he never gave up trying though. I was happy. We all were, although Olly's loss still lingered in the background for everyone. I could see it in their faces, and my health issues had only accentuated the frailties of my Family's emotional construct, but we had survived it all. After a long time, sunshine beckoned.

The entire summer in Pune was a breeze for me, interspersed with pre-monsoon showers, languid afternoons and charming evenings. The food was delicious and now my meals were getting regularized, albeit Beard still had to cheat to slip goodies to me stealthily while at the dining table. Politics suited him to a P. Mo was a relentless policewoman, her eyes darting around to ensure that neither Mama nor Beard had inadvertently dropped a paneer tikka that I had quickly gobbled up. Beard as you already know outwitted her in this cat-and-mouse game. Time flew literally like those pigeons in our Mumbai home; they disappeared in front of your eyes in a flash. They were gone. And before long we were scheduled to return to Mumbai. I wasn't very happy that no one had consulted me before taking such an epochal decision, but since I had a democratic spirit, I agreed to go with the majority view. But just because the majority feels one way does not make them right, kindly note. Might is not always right. I still remember Beard tugging at my chin and saying. 'Goodnight Lou, don't look so sad. We will be back again here soon.' Reassured, I slept like a dog.

It was like any other morning, except that there were more than a few scattered clouds on a largely quasi-warm day, the sun making a forlorn guest appearance overshadowed by the greying skies. I always found the monumental packing exercise quite hilarious. Big Mama, who is a natural born paragon of perfection, was like that maestro Zubin Mehta, issuing orders effortlessly that had to be diligently followed to the last tune. There was a raw nervous energy around, and I could see Beard watching the brouhaha from the balcony above, as usual grinning to himself. I hung around to make sure that all my core essentials, food tray, blue bed, medical supplies, and of course, my tennis balls were safely ensconced in what the humans call a 'dickey'. We were packed and ready for the return journey to our original home, Mumbai.

What happened next is a blur. Foggy images. Pardon my vague memory, please. Now my dear friend Pablo would always hyperventilate before any journey, sometimes out of FOMO, I think, as I mentioned earlier to you. Or maybe he felt he would be left behind alone. He was unrestrainable, like a loose cannon, even whimpering like a spoilt child every time before we travelled. I felt bad for him. I wanted to tell him that all was okay, we would be going home together as always, but in different cars. I therefore walked towards the back door of the big blue car to tell Pablo to just 'chill'. But what happened was something I was totally unprepared for. As was everybody else. All of a sudden, I saw my friend metamorphose into a dreadful incarnation, the kind I had never seen before. He seemed very angry with me, for no apparent reason. I was in fact coming to reassure him that all was fine. I had never seen Pablo so furious, not even in that gruesome altercation with Olly and me two years earlier. 'Why? What had I done? I was after all just coming to comfort him, to calm his atrocious insecure fears, for god's sake.' But then Pablo is Pablo, an incorrigible idiot of the first order. He rarely listened to anyone when he was inflamed. No one. Big Mama shrieked aloud, 'No!' But it was too late. I felt a piercing sharp stab in my stomach as Pablo's sharp teeth plunged deep into my tummy's soft texture tearing into them, before he flung me side to side in a fit of fury. At that moment, one goes numb. You feel everything and yet you feel nothing. All you know is that life is indeed so unpredictable, it can change so dramatically even in a nanosecond. I was motionless. Struggling. Blown out of my mind. In the distance, I heard the cries of everyone.

I lay looking above, watching my dear friend's face, a ball of uncontrollable madness merge with the grey skies. Then everything went black even as the cobbled-grey stones had turned red.

That is how I landed in the hospital.

15

HOME, AT LAST

'The way I see it, if you want the rainbow
you gotta put up with the rain.'
—Dolly Parton

I am not a valetudinarian, rest assured. I can live with all sorts of ailments, and not assume the worst. It is the humans who have become inveterate hypochondriacs after the virus. But lying in the dark, my mind a vortex of fuzziness, I was scared. For the first time in my life, I thought I was susceptible to something serious. 'Is this the way Olly felt too?' I am no control freak, but am independent-minded and like to navigate my own destiny. But right now, I did not know what was going on; I was in a stupor. And in terrible pain.

I was certainly not in Mumbai, my sacred home where I was all set to leave for. As I gradually began to get a whiff of what had transpired when the effect of those painkillers dwindled a wee bit, I knew that I was in an uphill battle now. It was easy to understand why. There is no way in heaven that my Family would ever let me be alone with these plastic, straight-faced, emotionless characters for whom I was just another dog; I was the Great Louis Jha after all, my Family's mascot-in-chief, their talismanic possession, the love of their lives. Their world revolved around me. They adored me. If they had left me in the custody of these grave-looking scammers, then it had to be, well, grave. It was. I craned my neck to see that I had some wretched scars on my stomach. I had apparently bled profusely, making me vulnerable to a multi-organ failure. The clinical readings were downright dismal; my kidney readings were indecipherable on those complex machines. The damn body is a terribly interconnected thing, like Mumbai's intractable traffic jam, that starts with one lousy traffic signal, and then percolates itself in various directions. But I was equally determined to survive this miserable ordeal. This was not going to be my obituary moment; Louis was meant to win the game, set and match. That brainless moron Pablo may have messed up big time, but there was no way I was giving up on my Family. I had to fight for them. I would give it my all.

Several hours had elapsed and on my mouth was a weird plastic mask that I am sure made me look like a scuba diver. 'Did I have Covid-19?' I hated it but I gathered that it was an oxygen mask; I was on life support. 'Jesus!' It was then that I at last saw my Family come through the door. Big Mama, Missy and Beard, their faces an avalanche of anxiety, trying desperately to hold back their tears. We looked at each other and I was dying to jump into Big Mama's arms and get straight back home, talk incessantly to Mo about my miraculous comeback from hell, and whisper to Beard that he should stop crying like a fool. If I could have been tongue-in-cheek, I would have told him, 'Don't sweat the small stuff, bro.' But this was hardly the place for our reunion, surrounded by a chubby, talkative doctor who appeared to control my destiny, who simultaneously spoke of both sky-high hopes and bottomless despair in one sentence. 'Huh?' It made little sense, honestly. He was clearly hedging his bets on me, and that was hardly comforting. But I was not going to give up. Economists talk of animal spirits; they had not seen mine yet.

We huddled together as a family, fully aware deep in our hearts that I was now beyond the marvellous miracles of modern science. All that I had was hope. Dreams. And our collective indomitable spirit. And of course, God. For the next few days, every time we parted at the hospital, we all gave each other long looks, unwavering attention, and endless words of love, as if anticipating that this was indeed the last farewell. Beard kept trying to hit the ceiling like a Jumping Jack on a sponge-bob to entertain me until Mama had to tell him to stop disturbing the other dogs. Obviously, that was an exercise in futility. Then on the fifth day at the hospital, life abruptly brightened up. I heard the talkative doctor say: 'Louis can go home the day after.' Why don't these doctors smile more often even when they have something cheerful to say for a change? They even share happy news with a morose countenance. They need to read Deepak Chopra, I think. It seemed too good to be true. I had survived a near-death experience, and although I still had a long road to recovery, it seemed that medically I was now completely out of the red zone. Providentially, I had pulled through. This was insane. It was beyond the pale of my wildest contemplations. I would indeed be back at our Pune home, forcing an extended holiday on everyone. Everything happens for a reason, right?

Round 1 to Louis Jha then; I was headed out of the wretched hospital. At last. I had survived Pablo's vicious assault. 'I would fire him later,' I resolved. Big Mama and

Missy came to pick me up on the day of my 'release' from the horrendous vet hospital, as excited as two schoolgirls going on their prom date. Mama appeared to be the younger one, judging by her hysterical behaviour. She couldn't stop smiling. Neither could I, although the morphine patch prevented me from going berserk with joy. Beard had seen me earlier, as he had to leave for Mumbai with Pablo, so that during my recovery period, I would not be distracted by some more gross misconduct on his part. 'No negative memories,' I heard him say. There was also the risk that I would start following him around too soon. But I wanted to see Pablo so much, because I had this visceral urge to slap him hard for being such a vagabond. What he did was so unnecessary and against the run of a winning play. 'My recuperation from my paralysis was nearly over, for god's sake, you buffoon!' I wanted to tell him. But 'you are forgiven' was the real message I wanted to convey to the irascible hunk.

By mid-afternoon, I was back at my lovely home. I could not believe it and neither could they. I heard our caretaker say 'Chamatkar' all over again. Magic was in the air. The whole house gave me a rousing welcome, and I could see Mama's methodical preparation for my grand comeback. Even the wet wipe napkins were kept at close proximity to my exclusive space on the sofa, so that I did not have to stretch at all. After surviving the detestable hospital, this felt like nirvana, a paradise. That's what home always meant to me. I cuddled in Mama's arms for hours and slept, and she did not move at all, not wanting to disrupt my snooze even for a bit. Mo kept teasing me with a tennis ball, and bouncing away like there was no tomorrow. I ate, walked a bit with help, and soaked in my return, still dazed by the events that had unfolded since mid-afternoon a week ago.

The afternoon sunshine streamed into my eyes, making me squint, and making the sadists laugh. I missed not seeing Beard; I had no idea that he was not there because he was doing his best to protect me. Left to him, Pablo and I would be separated forever now. We would live in two different homes in two different cities. The experiment with misplaced faith on the power of reconciliation between two disproportionately sized dogs was probably over in the Family's mind. Left to me, I could not imagine a life without seeing Pablo again. I loved him. Anyway, for the moment I thanked God. Truly there is someone up there who decides things, I think. It was too incredible this moment; I wanted it to be everlasting, uninterrupted. The nightmare was over. My second innings was about to begin.

Around ten o'çlock at night on the day of my fairy-tale return, all of us exhausted with both relief and the traumatic experience of the preceding days decided to go to sleep early for my sake. I couldn't wait to go back to my wonderland in Mama's blanket. I missed Beard that night. But I knew he would be back the next day, transporting along with him his boundless energy. I could do with an adrenaline rush. I wanted that. Missy had been painstakingly following up on my health and was so thrilled, I could feel her energetic reverberations from thousands of miles away. Mama and Mo gave me a million kisses, hugged me, and told me stories, and even at that late hour, they were willing to do the salsa dance to make me laugh.

My head was swimming with deliriousness. I tell you, I knew I was the luckiest furry animal in the world. The joy was overpowering. I joined Big Mama and Mo in the wild merriment even if I did not have the strength within me to match their hectic pace of bad Mexican dancing. This was party time. I smiled. I danced. I laughed. I loved. I cried. I laughed again. I remembered everything about my life. My sweet mother Lucy. Charlie. Olly. Bhola. Dr Rustam. Missy. Mo. Big Mama. Pablo. The expressway. Beard. I jumped. I swirled. I walked. I ran. I ran faster. I could not be stopped. I was on cloud nine. I was now flying, seeing the early manifestations of a galaxy I had not

HOME, AT LAST

even visualized before. I was out of control. Unknown to me and yet unknown to all, I had actually gone to sleep amidst the kinetic chaos. Not really, in scientific terms, I had gone into a coma.

So was this it then; curtains? Is this how it was meant to be? Is this the way it ends? My journey in this beautiful world with the world's loveliest cranky family was coming to the finish line. It will be silly of me to say with certitude what really happened, because I can only assume how it all played out in real time. Mama was inconsolable, Mo was totally broken, Missy in a fancy North American city was crying copiously for her little brother who had fought hard, refusing to surrender. And Beard, the man with the sanguine bug, who would even walk into a tsunami, broadcasting to the world that it was just an optical illusion, was perhaps driving back to Pune, still believing, still hoping, still praying that Louis and he would chase those tennis balls again. And that he would let me win. As he always did. I knew that. Even then.

Even as I perhaps remained motionless all of the following day, my breathing becoming shallow, I felt dog-tired, my small body giving way finally to only twenty seconds of madness of a week before, when I was all set to board the car for another wonderful journey on the highway. 'Oh, that feel of the breeze on my flying ears!' I remembered my life. 'Magical. Wonderful. Enchanting.' I had no complaints whatsoever. A journey that I was willing to do a million times more even if it ended the same way, with pain, suffering and loss at the end. We all die one day, but we are defined by the experiences of our journey. My Family was my world. I would take them with me wherever I went.

And then spectacularly out of nowhere, I woke up as if nothing had happened. Nothing. The accident was just a fictional blueprint of a warped mind. I was fine. Fit. Hungry. Ready to play. 'Where are you, losers, let's go!' I woke up for a fleeting second to say goodbye to them but both Big Mama and Mo were not watching, Beard was on a highway somewhere checking his watch anxiously as he returned home, and Missy was awake under her blanket thousands of miles away, praying while wiping her tears. 'I was going away for a bit only,' I wanted to tell them.

And then I was gone. Forever. It was 6.11 p.m. A Friday.

Louis Jha was dead.

16

A LETTER FOR MY FAMILY

'For when the One Great Scorer comes
To write against your name
He marks—not that you won or lost
But how you played the game.'
—GRANTLAND RICE

First and foremost, let me tell you that the famous Rainbow Bridge is not some imaginary, fabricated fantasy or something. It is for real. It has its own other-worldly appeal, no cars, no buildings, no pollution, no noise, no hospitals. No virus. Instead, it has white foamy clouds floating around, multicoloured homes with big gardens, several blue streams, toy shops, balls of different sizes, and sausage factories. Bathing is not on the menu card either.

I saw so many dogs, it was crazy. A German Shepherd was teaching a Chihuahua, sitting on his lap, to play the guitar, and a Rottweiler was being bullied by a Beagle for stealing his pork pie. A mini-Dachshund wrestled with a Pit Bull and pinned him down. Democracy reigned unlike what has been happening in many parts of the world. For a moment, I was totally befuddled, stunned by the speed at which I had come to this mysterious kingdom beyond. Jeff Bezos, Elon Musk and Richard Branson cannot achieve this supersonic speed, no matter how hard they try in their modern-day space capsules.

I was still feeling lonely and lost without my Family after twelve and a half mad years of togetherness, when I heard a familiar grunt and a gnarl. It was the same sound that had once welcomed me in 2009 after a hilarious car ride into the Family's home. I looked around everywhere and could not see anyone.

'Look here,' said the voice. And then suddenly at an angle of 55 degrees to my right was my darling soulmate, Olly. He looked the same, handsome, elegant, slightly grouchy and full of unkempt hair as always. He wore a pink polka-dot bow. There was no bruise on his back.

'I did not want you to come here soon, you fool,' he said, as we hugged, cried, laughed, and cried even more till our eyes had no tears left. It was heavenly being together again. Oh, how much I had missed his slurp and that Kung-fu master trainer look! A towering shadow soon emerged behind us that looked portentous. It turned out to be Amadeus, still possessing that majestic aura around him, like in the pictures I had seen framed in our home. He gave me a warm avuncular embrace, and I felt like a mayonnaise in a chicken burger. Sandwiched. We were family. I had one here too. And we were together. We exchanged notes, but I was surprised to know that they knew everything I had gone through. I was speechless. But I was furiously weeping, missing my Family like I would a fried omelette.

'Write to them,' said Olly and Amadeus together. 'It will make you feel better, trust us.'

They both wiped my tears dry with their long, wet kisses.

'Go ahead,' they said. 'We will fetch you in a bit. There is a grand reception for you here tonight. Lucky is singing Celine Dion's "I Am Alive" and Julie is doing a pole-dance.'

So I sat back on the lush green grass in a rose garden, surrounded by a rainbow and a soft undercurrent of breeze, and began to write letters to my Family.

Dear Missy

I know when you last saw me before taking off to your new home abroad, you had that awful premonition that you may not see me again. It always happens when you stay abroad, those nagging fears stay with you, like a haunting dark melody. I understood that. That is why during mealtimes you always made sure that I was on your lap, because you wanted to maximize every minute of your time here with me. Being away makes it unbearably harder especially when your boy is older and unwell. A sense of guilt inevitably creeps in. It is human. It is dog too, actually (can you see my smile?). I know that you will sometimes be harsh on yourself for what happened. But you are wrong. It was your compassionate and caring heart that resulted in Pablo's adoption by us. How many people really care for rescue dogs? Pablo would have been crushed under a wheel even before he was three months if you had not saved him. We must never lose faith in our goodness. Ever. Faith always wins over fear, remember that. And a good deed is a good deed. The outcome is not in our hands, but we must always believe in the impossible. Give Pablo the freedom to be in his own space. I think you truly understand his psychology best. Let sleeping dogs lie, and he will overcome his insecurities on his own. He will be extremely lonely for sure, and will need everyone's support to pull through this phase. And, by the way, don't forget to say a big hello to that adorable, captivating fellow called Miso that you adopted, who has now become a fashionable mascot where Big Mama works; a hero, a corporate talisman.

Relationships are hard work; they can be so easily destroyed. In a spur of a moment, frankly. But those who nurture them, also live with their imperfections, knowing fully well that we are all messed up somewhere. Expecting optimum relationship performance is like asking for the full moon thirty days a month. Even the gorgeous Jennifer Anniston knows that (I liked her in *The Morning Show*) it is not happening. By that rigid measure, how do we fare personally ourselves? Badly mostly, right? The answers to life's most difficult questions lie within us. Blaming others is convenient, but also escapist. Unlike us dogs, you all are multi-layered. Take the peel off and humans will see themselves as they really are.

But it takes courage. I know it is a cynical world you live in but don't lose trust in the goodness of people. Trust and do so unconditionally, albeit there will be advocates of unwarranted scepticism. Don't let the bitter experiences of the past make you cynical. Learn from it, or unlearn from the experience. There are more good people than bad, although everyone is entitled to their bad hair day in the office. Negativity will make prime-time news but the world moves ahead on the quiet decency of billions. Throughout my struggle, what kept me going was hope. Optimism, as some wise guy once said, is falling from the 60th floor of a building and when zooming down towards the walkaway at 100 mph and crossing the 36th floor, saying: 'So far, so good. Who knows, maybe Tobey Maguire might be around, right? Since that fellow with the funny face, a bodysuit with designer web and blue underpants rakes in billions, I am sure you guys believe in his preternatural appearances, don't you? Just hang in there.' The winner is always the one who just stayed longer, played that one last shot over the net. Please don't let people shame Pablo for what happened to O and me. There are always two sides to a story. Even if one side is 1 per cent right, it becomes a collective responsibility for both. I hope you will visit Pablo more often because he is not going to get younger as the years roll by. And you are and always will be his Big Mama.

I was hoping to be there when you get married to that abstract scientist-looking fellow from

California, who wears his cap in reverse, has a deep baritone voice, and loves funky music. He is a nice guy even if he likes cats more. I think he adores you, but tell him, he should have found more time for a lil' mini-D. Thanks for choosing me, Missy, the crackpot with a crooked tail. You wrote this story, Missy, otherwise there was no Lou. I am there always for you, and right now I can see you try and make a brilliant presentation on that Zoom call, looking like a cool pro in that dark business suit. I love you, Missy. I will tell everyone here that you are Exhibit A of kindness. Miss you always, and when you do too, just look up at the stars and you know I am there, hidden among the dazzling jewels in that cerulean sky.

༄

Dear Mo

This afterlife feels funny, to be honest. I know you dreaded this moment, but there it is. Our lives may be ephemeral but love can be everlasting. It is. And love is the most powerful emotion of all, isn't it? I think love is the cure for all of your toxic world's problems. But those who exhibit their feelings uninhibitedly are mocked at for being soft and sentimental. Being muscular and macho is in vogue.

Can I share a joke with you, Mo? Now I am actually feeling like how John Lennon must have felt. Why? I have no clue of what I did to deserve this sudden distance from you all. But that's the way it was meant to be, I guess. You are the kindest soul I know and have a very forgiving disposition. Pablo did not even remember what he did and why he did seconds after lacerating my tummy. Anger is a form of short madness after all, nothing more. I strongly recommend a prompt apology from the perpetrator of outbursts; it heals. If Pablo had met me and acted as if nothing had happened, I would have barked him down till he did. I know you will give him the love you had so circumspectly stored for me alone (my bad) before leaving for your studies abroad shortly. He is not a bad guy at all, he is just emotionally immature and frightfully insecure, which are his childhood issues. Please Mo, promise me you will help him heal because Missy will often be abroad, and I know Beard will take longer than most to reconcile to a world without me.

Anger is awful, as Pablo has probably taught us all. Long after you guys have cooled off and blamed your inflammatory outpourings on your house help for not giving you your cuppa on time or some such trivial nonsense, the hurt for the recipient lingers. Trust eviscerates

A LETTER FOR MY FAMILY

over a period of time, and those around you see you as a gremlin. Or a poltergeist. Don't treat anger management casually; it is tougher than making Pablo go for a walk with Bhola. You are a gentle soul and you must become an ambassador for love and compassion one day, even when your dad is cheering for his Liverpool team that you so hate.

With us dogs, what you see is what you get; we are not hypocritical like many among humans. The mirror has only one face where we are concerned. White supremacists in America asphyxiate Black Americans like George Floyd to death, but will want black cars and black dogs as a status symbol. Weird, no? We are not like that. We are straightforward.

I will miss giving you my long kisses on your nose on your post-graduation ceremony day in Manchester, my baby Mo, but when you are getting that amazing distinction, do look up at the sky once, and a mini-Me will be there wearing wings and clapping away, making the loudest cacophony. I will also miss your firing Beard when he cracks those inappropriate jokes at the dining table and was subjected to your copyrighted salvo: 'Boomer, there you go!' He deserves it for being cheeky. Well done. I played an adroit accomplished diplomat during these incongruous slugfests; did these banal outbursts between the boomers versus snowflakes really matter? I kept a straight face and looked both left and right, and chose to be a centrist instead. Neither woke nor a fossil.

Do I even need to tell you how much I miss

you, you monkey? And hey, by the way, tell your friends to smoke less (why don't you all eat more chocolates instead?). And even from up here, I will bat for Manchester City. And that funny fellow Novak. And that nerdy geeky boyfriend of yours, who seems to be in a Zen state at most times, like a little adorable Buddha of sorts. Love you, princess. I know you will shine bright always doing the innumerable good things you do for everyone quietly, unobtrusively. Spread the love. Bye bye Mo!

֎

Dear Big Mama

The whole of this great heavenly abode is not a match to your one hug, the comfort of your warm lap, the feeling of your closeness around me. I miss  you so much. Thanks to you I carried so much weight around the house, the tail literally wagged the dog, no? I know you try to be very strong, but it is okay to cry when you miss us, and miss me, in particular. Everything happened so suddenly we did not even get a chance to say goodbye the way we would have liked to. But I made it home, didn't I? And we spent the whole of my last night together like old times, even if I was so drugged out by then. I will never forget that day when I puked, pooed, and peed all over the bed all night and you took care of me without complaining even once. And you had a global conference to attend the next morning where you were one of the keynote speakers. And not surprisingly, you did a fabulous job of it. I was so proud of you that day, Mama, you have no idea.

All of us cope with grief differently; but I know it is hard. When grief checks in, it becomes a permanent guest. The only difference is that it soon becomes a part of family and no one notices it. But rest assured, it will give you periodic reminders that the bed needs to be done, the cupboard needs to be decluttered. I know how much all of you have cried in your private moments, each one trying to be brave for the other. And yet we heal with time, with beautiful memories that remain etched forever in our hearts. Life is impermanent, our memories though are perennial. I always thought that was just some corny maudlin stuff. After death, I know it is not. But why do humans not get this when they can still do something about it? Must one suffer to realize that life is beautiful, warts and all?

There are many who will blame Pablo for what happened. Tell them to go see a shrink. What happened between us was just a tragic accident. Unlike humans, we don't conspire to kill, we do not do mob lynching, or thrash someone mercilessly till they are dead. There are no hired assassins in our midst. Terrorists are what humans create. We are just sometimes carried away in a moment of weakness. Only to regret it forever. Sadly, my friend Pablo has had no closure with me. And deep down in his heart he is still looking out for me somewhere, anxiously waiting for my return. I know it is hard to forget that horrific moment because you were there when it happened, but I am glad you have shown such fortitude and forgiveness, Mama. It is only the strong who can do that. As Dale Carnegie famously said, don't criticize, condemn or complain. If everyone followed just that one principle of living, life would be a cakewalk. But it isn't. If humans can make peace with two facts, that life is both not fair and not easy, they will make a beginning.

I know work gives you a vertigo-like high, but you will agree, that I was your real gin and tonic, almost like a Molotov cocktail ready for action. I know you wake up sometimes at night and think of that small bundle that was constantly nuzzled against you. If you open the window curtains and look up at the stars, you will see me there, your little Louis now a twinkling star, your bodyguard in perpetuity. I will never let anyone ever harm you, Mama. This alpha-male with his biceps and triceps isn't going away anywhere. I love you.

Dear Pablo

I am so mad at you for unnecessarily ruining our beautiful if volatile friendship and life. I know you  were delighted with my quick rehabilitation because your walking partner was back. I know deep down inside you are devastated and you have no idea where I am because you were in Mumbai and I was in Pune when I was no more. What a blast we were having in Pune, chasing cats, eating grass (ours is a healthier version of what humans eat to get surreptitiously 'high'), getting into barking duels with that black Labrador whenever he crossed our home, walking freely without being held by Bhola on a tight leash, pooing behind that rose bush, and eating at the same time in that old-fashioned kitchen where the birds incessantly chirped.

I know you still look out for me, sitting in the balcony of the house, wondering where I am. We were three of us two and a half years ago, and now it's just you. It is not easy, but I have told the sweet Family to spoil you rotten, even if you don't deserve it as much. I have told them not to demonize you; instead, they should weaponize you with love. They will. You have no hate in you, Pablo, you are just an insecure, egoistic, fearful fool; that trinity is intertwined. Olly and I were older and smaller, that's why we were always more protected, more mollycoddled. Your pint-sized brain took that as a love bias; you became judgemental, allowing your better instincts to be overpowered by your negative emotions. But you will learn as we all do. And you will do better. The reality also is that they give a dog a bad name and hang him as the expression goes, but I am sure the Family will see you through this tough period. Hold on. I will be watching for you too, dimwit. I always had your back. The Family used to call me your Dog Mama, can you believe that?

I forgive you, my friend, despite the fact that I had to leave my Family so prematurely. It has been terribly hard, I must admit. Promise me one thing, you will work hard to stop people from casually indulging in their inflammatory outbursts. Remember, anger destroys relationships, and all we can do is regret thereafter. But the damage is done. Words are like toothpaste, once out of the tube, it cannot be put back.

Look after my Family, Pablo, and keep them safe. Despite my small size you know I would have died for them. You must do the same now. I love you, bro. Stay there. I don't want to see you in a hurry.

Dear Beard

I am addressing you in the end because I know you are a gargantuan disaster; even Missy and  Mo will handle my going away better than you. You need to grow up. You are the one who lectures the universe on handling tough times, etc., so now practise it yourself. Facing the inevitable with tenacity and valour is what you have always inspired others to do. In fact, those lessons helped me so much through my last few days. I kept fighting. You made me believe in the impossible. You are a diehard optimist, one who never gives up hope. Sometimes your faith in the infinite possibilities of miracles can unnerve some, but what is life if we do not believe in the magic of the unknown, the unprecedented? Like the rainbow behind the huge mountains after a torrential downpour in Thimphu, you remember? Or the amaranthine ocean that never stops even as the evanescent rays of the sleepy sun bids adieu? Aren't they miracles that we never pause to imbibe? So, Beard, don't stop being that spirited crazy fellow that you are. Be yourself, bald head, grey stubble and getting thrashed on TV every day and all that. I am sorry but now it is my time to preach. You can't teach an old dog new tricks for a reason—because we know them all. Just listen to my lecture carefully.

First, you have to forgive Pablo from the bottom of your heart, and not just to please the girls. Why don't you google and see the photographs of Adolf Hitler, Benito Mussolini and Osama bin Laden when they were four years old? They were paragons of innocence and simplicity, with not a trace of anger or hate in them, right? They were like any of the millions of other children of that age. Today the world remembers them as heinous murderers who perpetrated horrors for pursuing some twisted agenda. As humans, we need to understand what went wrong in between that phase of running with the rabbits and chasing kites and preparing for a cold-blooded massacre of helpless civilians in a concentration camp. Or in an airplane. The villain is often the victim, Beard. Of circumstances, of bad company, of distorted education, of unpleasant experiences, of pernicious propaganda, of brutal betrayals. Nothing can absolve them of their beastly behaviour, but life is complicated, Beard. We don't live in a black-and-white world; the shades of grey are large and omnipresent. Fifty shades, eh? Remember, Nathuram Godse once played with toys too, and James Earl Ray drooled for a chocolate icecream. If hate can infiltrate our minds so

A LETTER FOR MY FAMILY

can love permeate our being. And so never forget that Pablo once was the most docile silly-billy who needed our shelter and security. If we had not given him our home, you would have lived your whole life feeling guilty about where he was, whether he even survived a week on the bustling streets of Mumbai. He will do well, I know.

Dude, the only way out for you poor humans, your only hope to move forward is forgiveness. Keep the grudges, resentments and hate brewing within, and soon you will have wrinkles, a bloated tummy, dark circles under your eyes, and you will be passing wind silently sometimes, and loudly at others, as you will face a gas crisis, worse than the one caused by the Ukraine war.

For sure, castration is an awful idea to calm a hot-headed guy's temper. You guys are barking up the wrong tree in the hope that it has a mellowing effect. When couples go to see a marriage counsellor, does he recommend hacking off the man's balls to mollify his rage, Beard? Where you guys probably go wrong is in assuming that mental health does not affect us (seriously, we are more intelligent than you duffers). Can you smell the other from miles away? (And I am not referring to your sweaty armpits, please.) Pablo needed to see a therapist (by the way, unlike some of you we won't attach any stigma to being open about it, rest assured) and you all should know that. You should have known that given the fact that he shivered and trembled outside the house, fearful and frightened of the unknown, when he went out for walks. Or when guests arrived, he retreated behind us with Ol and me becoming his security guards, two Lilliputians being the guardrail of a terrified Hulk. But you missed it.

You humans are not the only ones suffering from behavioural issues; me thinks Pablo had a bad case of PTSD, which was aggravated by him feeling that at home he was given a step-brotherly treatment. Olly and I knew that, y o u all did not. Sorry, but facts are facts. Psychological security isn't just your thing, folks. So be nice to the hot-head. Promise me that. I think now that we are both gone, he will have no one to fight with. His insecurity will vanish. He  will be okay. Although, trust me, neither Ol nor I had to be part of a shit show experiment for his mental rehab. But that's life.

The childhood derangement of being torn away from his parents and left to die perhaps was Pablo's perennial hallucination. You all underestimated that, surprisingly, despite knowing that he was a serial offender at home, where lil Olly and I became his easy targets of suppressed aggressive outpourings. Sometimes Olly and I did discuss this between us: why is the Family so oblivious of a clear and present danger? But then I guess we are all hard-wired to believe that nasty things don't happen to us. The therapist knows otherwise, and they do what most humans don't: they listen to you without interruption, trying to understand the dark cobwebs in brittle heads. Like us only. Consequently, you know you are being heard and respected for your feelings. No one is passing judgements on your alleged irrationality and dreadful tantrums, blah blah. You humans would be great therapists for each other if only you were less egocentric. If you only tried to listen and understand the other. All Pablo needs is to be appreciated with all his innumerable faults and helped along the way with abundant love. For you to understand his deep-rooted anxiety which requires your empathetic understanding. He is not a case of permanently damaged goods, for heaven's sake. He needs your forbearance and forgiveness. Forgiveness is a protein shake for our emotional muscles, it absorbs shocks with insouciant resilience. Anger, however, atrophies it. It debilitates your soul, destroys its real self through manufactured resentments and imaginary phantoms. I kept seeking rapprochement with the scoundrel despite our intermittent issues because reconciliation is the only way to be. Deepak Chopra would call it an 'atomic realignment' perhaps. Pablo behaved like a rogue, but I knew that he was a victim of a seriously disturbed past. But I do wish the cranky chap knew that black lives matter. Anger and fear are inextricably intertwined as the cliché goes. Fear is also interestingly described as tilting at the windmills. But those who fear are those who usually live in the future but base the uncertainty of what might happen tomorrow on past experiences. Hey, how about living now, in this very second that you are reading this lengthy monologue of mine?

Give me gratitude over grudges any day. Bygones are bygones is what you all frequently say, and yet you betray your own platitudes. We dogs don't conspire to hurt, and we don't spend billions to annihilate each other through nuclear bombs. We don't get into a herd and thrash a fellow from our fraternity because of our seething rage. We are instinctive, spontaneous, and express ourselves sometimes terribly, but we are not wilful murderers. Don't label Pablo. You won't allow anyone to ever do that is something you must promise me. One day you will be proud of Pablo. Remember the famous maxim: love me love my dog? Start with tolerating our quiet farts and inscrutable mood swings. One day Pablo will get old, forlorn and immobile. One day my sweet friend will die too. No regrets this time, please, Beard.

You know when you tattooed me on your left forearm I was over the moon (it is closer from here). I knew you would do something like that. Are you the only politician in the whole world with a dog's tattoo? The Guinness Book awaits you, Beard. I know you will forever seek redemption: why didn't you anticipate the worst? If you had just picked me up a bit earlier. Why did we all have to go together on that particular day that you had taken the E-Pass for, etc.? It is okay, I understand that, but finding inner peace is about acceptance. It is easier said than done but it removes guilt, bitterness and remorse. How do you get all determined to fight back after losing a close match on the tennis court? Follow that same resolution. That same determination, Beard. You can do it. You often said quoting a self-help messiah that if life gives you a lemon, make a lemonade. Well, you boring teetotaller, put some vodka in it too. You can do with a drink.

I want to say a big thank you for being around me all the time when I stopped walking. I know you were broken and bushed, but you looked after me so well, your love gave me the strength to believe in my resurgence, my comeback. It had to happen. It did. Those walks, cleaning my poo in the garden, both of us in the swimming pool, wearing those Ivy-league sweaters in Pune's cold that made me look like a Harvard research scholar, following me when I went all over the place, it was so beautiful. I felt so loved. I was never made to feel like a burden that you had to endure. You never leaving me alone, and giving me those exercises religiously, they made my last year a wonderful journey in knowing the man who first spotted my doppelganger at the Race Course, and then went on to start this most bewitching journey ever, an emotional roller-coaster ride even a Disney musical fantasy can't match.

You used to call me Louis XV because you

wanted me to live for at least that many years, but you know what? That French emperor was also considered a benevolent and beloved emperor, so thanks for that unintended compliment, Beard. I am glad you wear your emotional vulnerability on your sleeve; it is a sign of strength, and I blithely endorse that. Very few are blessed with the courage to face their fears, you know. Props to you for that.

I know you are a sentimental idiot; an emotional song from the past will get your tap-work flowing. Or on reminiscing about me rummage through the basket of balls in the far corner of the living room. You were particularly enchanted by the disciplined soldier who obeyed your commands by walking parallel to the long hallway after a night out of hooliganism, sheepishly ignoring eye contact. Or basking in refulgent glory in the summer sun in the extended balcony, my siesta interrupted only by the doorbell's exasperating intrusion. Or your indulgent look when my small buttocks turned the corner and disappeared from your optical vision (see, I knew it all along).

It is okay, as I know that despite the unending supply of goodies here in heaven, I will often get the blues too. It is going to be hard; I will miss the madness and mayhem that only my unhinged family can so effortlessly conjure.

And lastly, something I told you even when we were physically together but I think you never heard, because you are always looking confused, battling conundrums in your head. In that last year, we developed a bond that was so heart-rending, our eyes said it all through that challenging struggle. So, it's time I told you: Thank you, Dad. You are the father I always wanted. My Charlie. I love you, Beard (please trim more often, faux Karl Marx). And hey, Dad, remember the ending of one journey is a must for the beginning of another. Maybe our story can be called Me and You and a Dog named Lou (unoriginal, but cool, right?).

If I have sounded like a self-help guru, it is all your fault (don't take it personally, I am including 8 billion of you in this). You guys never help yourselves, quibbling over trivial codswallop you will not even remember a week later, but in your moments of tumultuous temperamental deluge, you make every molehill become an Amazonian climb. The worst thing is this atrocious paranoia to have the last word. If you guys just knew the importance of shutting up, you would find that despite megalomaniacal dictators, melting glaciers, social media verbiage, and crazy guys carrying guns into school campuses, life is still beautiful. Because there are so many who are selflessly working hard to stop the chaos too. Life is not perfect, far from it, I concede but it is foolish to expect it to be otherwise. Agree? If you don't, your bad, dad.

Take care of Missy and Mo, and Big Mama. I hope after me you guys will fight even more for #BlackLivesMatter (chuckle chuckle). Because my sermons apart, I know this is going to be hard. Grief has no closure; it only has an endurance.

Enough for now. I better go as I am the chief guest for the sumptuous dinner and dance party that awaits me. I can't keep the senior citizens, Ol and Amu, waiting, can I?

You promised me a walk in that Race Course, remember? That is still pending, Dad. I will therefore have to be back (can you see my wink?) to make that unfinished dream happen. And I think you know that.

Goodbye! Miss you all so much.

EPILOGUE
ONE MONTH LATER

*'The key to immortality is first
living a life worth remembering.'*
—Bruce Lee

It is a month since Louis passed away (I prefer saying this to 'died' for some strange inexplicable reason). The car fully packed, we begin the drive to Pune, a mere three hours away from Mumbai at moderate speed. Missy is at work abroad and Big Mama and Mo are visiting an ayurdevic resort in south India for some rejuvenation therapy. Pune was Louis' favourite destination in the final year of his life. The last time we drove out, he was in the back seat, looking out of the window like a visiting head of state acknowledging the greetings from crowds standing and waving at him from the wayside. This time I have Pablo, who as is his customary behaviour, is feverishly excited. After a while, he calms down. The car cruises along a melancholy charcoal-coloured road, interspersed with tunnels that look like bloated caterpillars with a hollow stomach.

As we hit the six-lane expressway the car accelerates further, and this was the time Louis would settle in for a long sleep till suburban Pune would wake him up, the car crawling, and the city traffic adding to the hullabaloo. I look outside my window and configure Louis among the clouds; that one, above the Khandala ghats looks like him sitting to eat, while the one right in front of the sightscreen is his adorable ears flapping as he runs. Right through the journey, I see him amidst the surroundings, a black dog running across a temple in a faraway field deserves a second look. But he is there somewhere. The smoke emanating from the old engine of the decorated but dilapidated truck torturously pushing ahead on a snaky highway in front of our car creates a cloudy image of Louis looking sideways, a wee bit piqued perhaps for being denied a snooze in the back seat. Or on my lap. The journey belongs to him. I can think of nothing else.

I am flooded with his memories; his mad, capricious ways; the early morning wake-me-ups that would bring him to ultimately lick my face while I pretended to be asleep, his hot body which I would tuck inside my blanket when it got cold thus not allowing him to escape my giant clasp of his small frame. His emphatic monopolistic capture of my lap when I would write on my study table, his eyes squinting at my Word document, often disapproving of my sentence construction. Perhaps the most delightful of all, trying to take a ball out from under the sofa by swimming sideways, his short legs, now pepper and salt as he had got older, frantically doing the freestyle. That was trademark Louis. The pursuit of a ball gave him an inconceivable high. When he got acutely lonely, he would surprise me: either he waited right outside the bathroom till you came out of your shower or he would sit with you past the midnight hour when you had finished inking your latest manuscript. Louis never left you alone. My last memory of him of that fateful day is looking at me intently through his now cataract eyes, a caramel tinge in them, asking me to help him up the sofa, where he sat while I gulped down my breakfast hastily. We were to leave for Mumbai in an hour, and I still had to pack. Louis never made it. Was that his final goodbye to me then, did he have a premonition of his death? Was he saying 'Hey Beard, I am sorry' to me?

We reach Pune and it appears that I am not just at home but have come to say hello to Louis, letting him know that we never left him alone in the backyard where he now rests with Olly and Amadeus. The sky is slightly overcast, the grass is grown longer and thicker, the front door is ajar and I half-expect him to poke his face out from the drawing room inside, and say: 'Where the hell were you, Beard?' The caretaker gives me a wan smile, telling me perhaps that he understands what I am thinking. Outside, I hear a few dogs squabbling away. Pablo joins them as they make unparliamentary introductions, his toned, muscled body matching his imperious snarl. The birds are sounding mellifluous, perhaps delighted by the seasonal showers. A friendly neighbour waves his hand. I wave back and smile. The evening is setting in, and Pablo scampers all over the house, perhaps looking for his little friend of whom there is no sign. There is no trace of any blood on the pebbled pathway either. It seems as if nothing has changed. And yet everything has. In a few moments, it is sunset. My shadow follows me inside the house like an energetic black sausage once did.

I walk to the rear of the house, where Louis now lies

buried with his two friends. The patch of ground above is muddy; it has been raining heavily in Pune. The little green sampling that was planted there has grown and has been weathering storms resolutely. I know Louis is fine. He is resting, his one small leg always suspended in mid-air, his eyes closed like a child imagining a balloon ride into the skies, a picture of peace and grace. Always. Painless at last. I recollect Emily Bronte's *Wuthering Heights* as I think of the three occupants underneath in the ground below me; together they have given us thirty-six years of unbridled love: 'I lingered round them, under that benign sky; watched the moths fluttering among the heath, and hare-bells; listened to the soft wind breathing through the grass; and wondered how anyone could ever imagine unquiet slumbers for the sleepers in that quiet earth.' I imagine Louis, Olly and Amadeus together burrowing an underpass below, and engaging in a nocturnal rendezvous; chatting, playing, and generally conspiring their return. They were capable of anything. Did I notice the earth move or was it just a flurry caused by a monsoon windstorm?

I stand there in silence for a few minutes, a homage that could be interminable for all I care, and then head upstairs and start unpacking my bags. I have a deadline for an article submission to an online magazine that I must wrap up by late evening, so my laptop takes precedence over everything else. The terrace is driving a cool current of breeze inside and I am compelled to ask for some ginger tea in a hurry. The laptop flickers and then after what appears like an eternity the document file opens. Outside I can hear the familiar thunder that presages a heavy downpour. The season has changed. It is a new month. Life, that one pertinacious machine that never takes a break, plods ahead. Unstoppable. Suddenly I hear a giant thud; startled, I look back to see that the caretaker has tripped and fallen while lowering my tennis bag on the makeshift rack.

'Sorry,' he says, but I do not hear him. I hear nothing. Because all I can see and hear is a yellow Wilson ball rolling on the floor, disconsolate and doleful, that no one is giving it a chase of a lifetime. That no one is huffing and puffing, and then hoisting it up like a trophy won in its clenched mouth. The ball settles in the middle of the floor, unattended, looking as grief-stricken as me. I start to cry. I cannot stop the tears flowing. I take a deep breath, overpowered by feelings that I seem to have no control over. The op-ed article on a nation torn apart by communal polarization must wait. It has to. I turn to face my laptop awaiting my keyboard commands, the cursor flickering as if hastening me to do what I must, and begin to write a story, the story of the most beautiful boy I have ever known, a boy who taught me love like no other.

'I grew up in a crowded home with three cantankerous...'

ACKNOWLEDGEMENTS

The moment the book wrapped up, I did what is now becoming customary when I complete writing a story; I sent it to my friend, the enigmatic Kapil Komireddi, who is a natural born iconoclast. I am an unabashed addict of his brilliant prose. Kaps has a generous bone and thus habitually indulges me—and quite liberally—to be honest. After reading the whole manuscript, he tweeted that I had written a potential blockbuster. Blockbuster or pure bunkum, the book needs a publisher first. That is how I was fortuitously connected to one of India's most established literary agents, the ubiquitous Kanishka Gupta.

Kanishka is a unique blend of endless patience and energetic passion for books but possesses an exasperating forgetfulness when it comes to reading his emails. But seriously, he is a gem of a human being, who makes you feel like he is representing William Shakespeare. I am hugely grateful that I met him. Courtesy Kanishka's pursuits in search of a perfect partner, I have ended up working with the wonderful Rupa Publications. I have worked with several editors in the past (and they have all been fabulous), but since this book is a deeply personal one, I was anxious that I had an empathetic guide, someone who would understand my journey. In Dibakar Ghosh I was fortunate to have found an editor who understood and cared to read between the lines and look beyond the text. He did not have to cajole me much to see the literary merits of his suggestions (which have truly enhanced the read, in my opinion) even as he generously respected the idiosyncratic stubbornness of writers who are mostly obsessed with 'author's identity'. I owe Dibakar my sincerest appreciation for being the perfect lighthouse.

As I desperately looked for an illustrator to better represent Louis' eccentricities, Bhavya popped up. Despite her globetrotting schedule and pressing project engagements, she happily acquiesced to working with me. But when she said 'I am so glad to be part of Louis' journey', I was both emotionally overwhelmed and secretly thrilled. If this book is able to give you a sense of the pathos and pandemonium in its story, full credit to this talented creative artist.

The caretaker of my Pune home, Deepak Dhokchawle, has no idea whatsoever of how much his ginger tea with dollops of milk and half-teaspoon of sugar inspired me to write even when both the body and spirit was unwilling, broken as it was. Pablo remained a faithful companion during that period, completely unaware, that he was himself going to be on the bookshelves soon.

Lastly, a huge shout-out to my family—Pallavi, Maithili and Mohini—who understood that I was incorrigibly distraught and beyond the realms of hope and treatment, and just let me be, while quietly praying that I would find my peace somehow, sometime. They are very strong, lovely souls—and maybe I should say this more often to them—take a bow, ladies!